I0714346

Holding On

Also By

Broken Together

Thick Chicks

Engaged

Let Me Love You

A Christmas Kiss

SHORT FICTION

Hallway Lights

Daily Bread

Jack & Diane

The Ride

The Honeymoon Journal

Holding On

A NOVELLA

K.L. GILCHRIST

ISBN-13: 978-1-7341705-3-5

eBook ISBN-13: 978-1-7341705-2-8

The author confirms that *Holding On* is a work of human imagination and lived experience. No generative artificial intelligence (AI) was used in the writing of this manuscript. The cover art and interior design were produced by human creators.

Scripture is taken from *The Holy Bible, English Standard Version® (ESV®)*, copyright © 2001 by Crossway, a publishing ministry of Good News Publishers.

Editing provided by Alicia Suber.

Cover design by Stefanie Fontecha for Beetiful Book Covers.

Interior design by Infinite Solutions Group, LLC.

Version_3

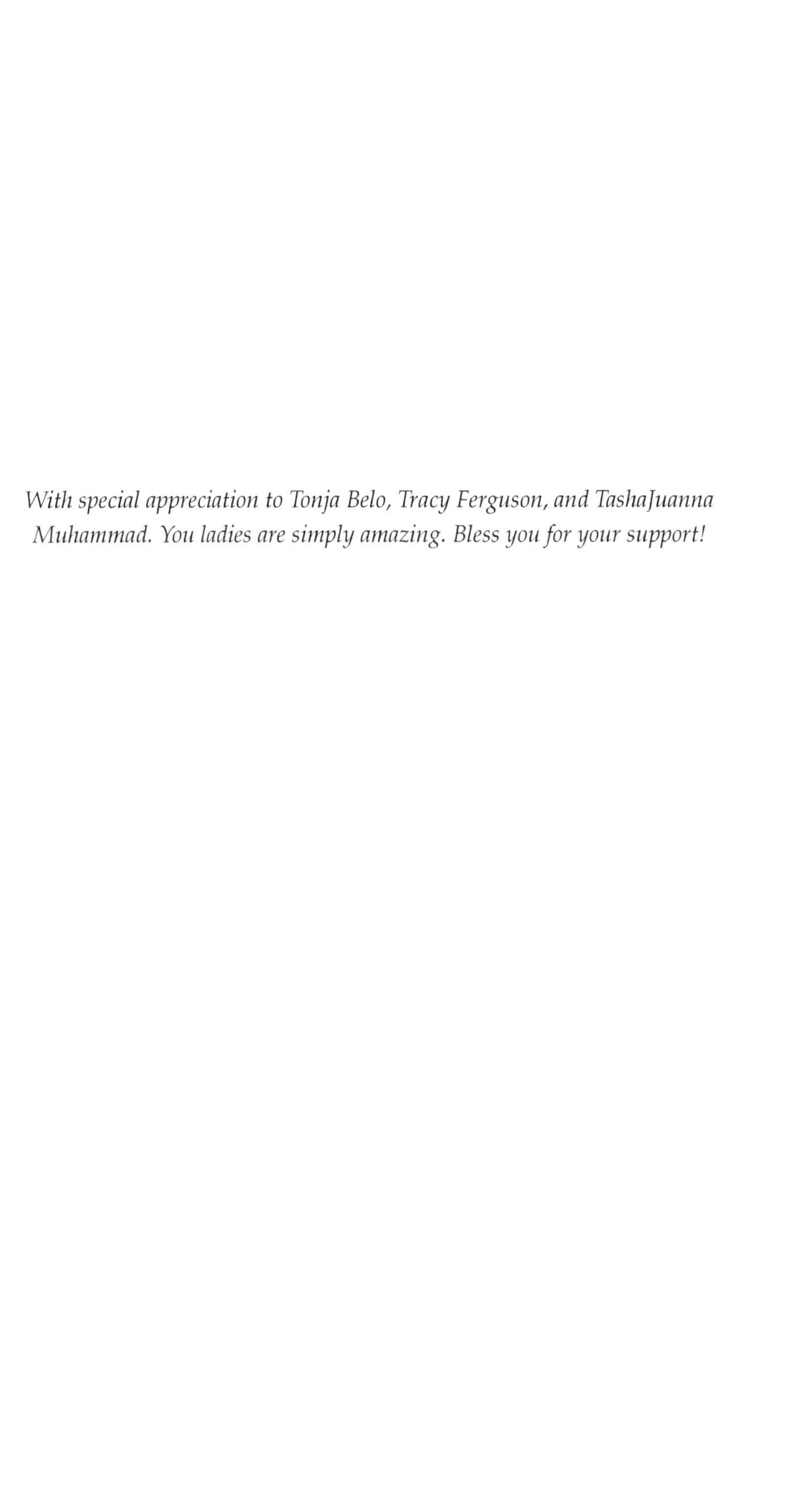

With special appreciation to Tonja Belo, Tracy Ferguson, and TashaJuanna Muhammad. You ladies are simply amazing. Bless you for your support!

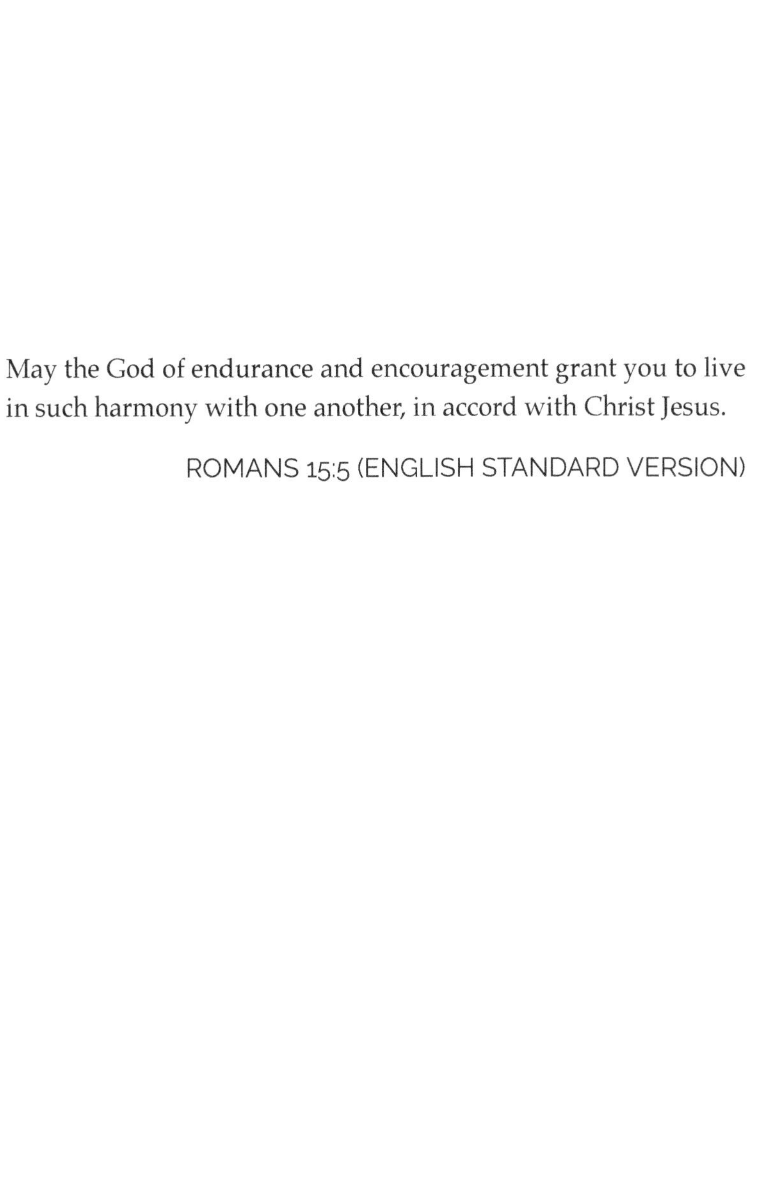

May the God of endurance and encouragement grant you to live in such harmony with one another, in accord with Christ Jesus.

ROMANS 15:5 (ENGLISH STANDARD VERSION)

CHAPTER
One

HOW WOULD SHE TELL HIM?

Maybe she could slip it in right after they ordered dessert? Something surprising they could discuss at the table? Unexpected of course, but Tracey and Brian Jones had experienced all types of situations in the history of their marriage. What words should she use? Nothing came to mind. Not while she visited the bathroom for the third time since they'd been seated at Talula's Garden. The whole time she washed and dried her hands, she chanted to herself. *Think of something.*

The toilet flushed behind her. A stall door opened and an older lady with short white hair sauntered out. She stood in front of the sink next to Tracey, running water then scrubbing her hands with soap. Tracey pulled a compact from her black clutch and began to touch up her makeup.

"You look fantastic, sweetheart." The lady chuckled. "Not a hair out of place."

Tracey gave a half-smile. "Thanks."

"I saw you two tables away from us in the restaurant. Having dinner with your husband tonight?"

"Yes."

"My he's a handsome one. Married long?"

"Almost thirteen years now." Tracey put her compact away. "Some friends told us about this place. I didn't want to wait until our next anniversary to visit."

The lady nodded, moving toward the bathroom door. "Well, you can come back then as well. My daughters and I eat here often. You have a good evening."

"You too."

Their next anniversary. Number thirteen. Tracey didn't believe in good luck or bad luck. But really, should they even acknowledge number thirteen? Or would they skip it or pretend it was fourteen or a revamp of twelve? Maybe call it twelve the sequel? The corners of her lips quirked into a light smile as she rubbed cherry-scented hand lotion into her palms. Brian and Tracey Jones. Thank God, they'd made it this far. Not without trouble, but they'd weathered the storms together. If happily ever after existed, she and her husband were living it.

Outside the bathroom, she stepped with care across the hallway and down the wooden stairs. Her brand-new heels had a slick bottom and the last thing she wanted to do was slip and fall. So far it had been a fabulous night for the Joneses. Together in the city. Peeking in the glass windows of Jeweler's Row. Chatting with one another and holding hands as they walked through the restaurant's lush garden outdoor eating area, admiring the strings of glittering lights on the wall. Sitting at a table for two, sharing their appetizer. Brian had ordered shrimp and scallops for his dinner. Tracey had requested the roasted duck breast. Everything tasted amazing.

With dinner over, she could go back and tell him her news and they could order dessert to go. They could eat it later after they made love. Yes, that's it. A wonderful way to end the evening.

At the table, Tracey sat down opposite Brian. "Miss me?" She grinned at him.

His voice sounded heavy. "It depends."

She peered in his face. Blank look. No smile. Slack shoulders.

"What's the matter? What happened?" She asked.

"Oh, I don't know what happened." He crossed his arms and pressed his back against his cushioned seat. "But right about now you need to tell me how long you've been texting Kyle."

Kyle Addison. Tracey's son Tyler's father. Brian had spent the last twelve years tolerating Kyle, and now with Tyler out of the house and attending Hofstra University, Kyle's name never came up in conversation. Tracey didn't talk about him and Brian didn't ask. But Brian had never been the type of person to supervise Tracey's phone habits, and that was the only way he could have discovered those texts.

"You've been on my phone?"

"You left it sitting right on the table. I heard it going off, so I picked it up. Turns out Monica's texting you pictures from her conference in Seattle. We hadn't heard from Tyler in a while, so I scrolled down your message list to see if you got anything from him today and I saw Kyle's name."

Tracey's face grew hot. "You're spying on me now?"

"How is it spying when we have no secrets? I know your passwords and codes and you have mine. Because we don't have anything to hide, correct?"

She gripped her water glass tight in her hand. She couldn't find the words to respond. That was what they'd agreed to years before. To be accountable and open with one another about everything. Protective of their marriage at all times and respectful of one another. She hadn't said anything about exchanging texts with Kyle. Brian had a right to be upset.

He shook his head and whistled. "I guess it's your turn to sleep in the office now?" He raised an eyebrow. "I mean, isn't that where cheaters have to sleep in our house?"

"A handful of texts does not equal cheating. That's not fair."

"You texting your baby daddy on the down low? That's fair?"

"He hasn't been my baby daddy for some time now. The last time I checked, that baby is a college freshman with a job and car."

"And you just proved my point."

"What point?"

"That there's no reason at all for you to be in contact with Kyle. The child you share is grown. What do you need to talk about with him?" Brian paused. He stared right in her eyes. "Unless you just like texting him."

The air shifted around Tracey. She dropped her head down, looking at her empty plate and the butcher block table beneath it. Moving her gaze to the right, she saw a couple trying hard to look like they weren't hearing snippets of Tracey and Brian's conversation. To her left a waiter approached. And in front of her? No, she would not look up. She'd be staring straight into Brian's eyes again. She couldn't do that. Not now, anyway.

The waiter reached them. "Are we ready to enjoy dessert tonight?"

Tracey didn't see Brian as he answered for them. "No, thank you. You can bring us the check please."

"Were the meals to your liking?" The waiter asked.

"The food was excellent." Brian said. "The food isn't the problem."

Whatever wasn't being spoken, the waiter seemed to understand. "I'll bring your check right away."

"Thank you."

Tracey swallowed at the lump in her throat. Stupid. She should have stopped with the prayers. She didn't have to text to check on Kyle. And why on earth was she sending him scripture? Sure, nothing bad appeared in any of those messages. Actually, she could have printed them all out and dropped them in front of Brian. All he would have read was a collection of *How are you doing? How are you holding up? Still praying for your father. Here's a link to Psalm 23. Focus on God's greatness and goodness* texts followed by *I'm holding up fine. Today I'm not doing so well. Thank you for your prayers. The scripture helps me. I'm just not ready to lose him* responses.

It was the principle of the thing. Brian promised he wouldn't privately contact other women. Tracey committed herself likewise regarding other men. She'd never had a problem holding up her end of the deal. Now though?

"I don't know what to say," She pulled herself upright, finally meeting her husband's gaze dead-on. "Did you read through all of them?"

"Of course, I did." Brian dropped his cloth napkin next to his plate. Half his dinner remained cold in front of him. "You were in the bathroom a long time."

"Well?"

"Wasn't much to them."

"I told you."

"Except the last one."

"What last one?"

Brian picked up Tracey's phone from the table, tapped her passcode then turned the device so she could view the screen. "Go ahead. Bring up your messages."

Tracey took the phone and tapped Messages, then tapped Kyle's name. There was a new message from him right there on the screen. No mistaking it.

"Want to read out loud for me?" Brian asked.

What good would it do to resist? She read aloud. "When you visit Tyler next time, can you meet me for coffee?"

Tracey's heart beat so fast she reached up and patted her chest. She needed to calm down. There wasn't anything to the coffee thing, Brian had to know that. But this type of message? Dangerous territory.

He leaned in. "First of all, why isn't he trying to have coffee with his own women?"

"Kyle is in crisis. His father is dying. He wants to talk to someone grounded. Someone who knew his father before Parkinson's."

Brian's fingertips drummed the table. "Honestly, I'm sorry about Judge Addison and I pray for their family, but..." He stopped for a second, then continued. "What if this were my phone? Turn the tables, Tracey."

She didn't have to.

She still remembered the way her stomach twisted itself in knots the day she'd discovered all those private phone calls and texts between Brian and his former nurse, turned lover, Lisette. Tracey had shaken with anger and frustration. Worse than that, she'd wondered if her husband had been stolen right out from beneath her nose. What a rough road they'd had to travel. Now it was all in the past, but only after months of counseling, prayer, and hard relationship work.

Tracey reached for her husband's hand. He let her touch him but didn't move any closer to her. Instead, he looked away.

"I am so, so sorry. But you know me," she told him. "You scanned the texts. Don't read into it something that isn't there."

Silence.

"We've come too far. Those messages were some encouragement texts not worth mentioning."

More silence.

"Why in the world would I start something with him?" Tracey lowered her voice. "You and I both know I had the chance years ago. I wasn't willing to pursue anything then and I'm not willing now."

The hardness in Brian's face seemed to melt. He clutched her hand.

"Two weeks ago in life group. You asked for prayer for an unspoken item. I have to know. Was that request for Kyle?"

The unspoken prayer request. Tracey remembered Brian raising his eyebrows in their life group meeting that night, but he didn't ask her about it later. She looked at him now and couldn't lie.

She gripped his hand back, determined to hold on. "Yes."

Brian released her hand and reached for his wallet. When the waiter arrived, he plunked down his bank card. No further conversation as they waited for the receipt. When it arrived, he signed it, stood up abruptly, helped Tracey with her chair, and off they went out of the restaurant.

Away from the building, Tracey reached for her husband's arm again. He stopped walking but averted his eyes from her face.

"All I did was pray for him and encourage him." She moved in front of her husband, halting him from walking away.

Brian stepped so close to Tracey she could feel his heart thumping. He leaned down until his lips touched her ear. "You slept in that man's house! His house. While you were married to me. You're my wife. If he needs prayer, churches and prayer groups exist on Long Island. You can't serve as his private prayer partner."

He turned away from her then, moving with long strides down the block. He crossed Walnut Street then kept going past The Bible House. Tracey struggled to keep up. She reached his side when he stopped as a trio of motorcycles turned in at Sansom Street. Fumes blew in their faces, mixing with the smell of motor oil, street dirt, and city sewers holding filth flowing beneath their feet. Unseen, but still in existence.

They walked toward Chestnut Street in a different fashion than before their dinner. Space remained between their bodies. But this was supposed to be a celebration.

She needed to tell him. Now.

"Stop. Please, just stop!" She pushed a hand against his chest. "I need to say something."

Brian finally ceased moving. His nostrils flared. "Go ahead."

"I'm pregnant."

Tracey studied his face, catching the faintest movement of his lips. A potential smile? She hoped but didn't know for sure.

No blinking when his eyes finally met hers. "Are you sure it's mine?"

"I DIDN'T MEAN IT. I wish I could take back those words," Brian whispered in Tracey's ear.

She suppressed the urge to flick her fingers at him, forcing him to move his lips away from her face. He'd rolled over in bed and now he was trying to spoon. She stayed still and allowed his body to remain close, but didn't say anything back. Though it was nice to hear he didn't mean what he'd said while they were in Center City, frustration and anger still simmered inside her.

Especially since he hadn't said much to her for the remainder of that night.

Or for the following two days.

He'd been rigid, only communicating as much as necessary for a spouse in a household. *Yes, it's fine if you take Brianna with you to choir practice. I'm sending a contractor over to look at the hot water heater next Tuesday at ten. No, I don't want to go to dinner at Charla and Ricky's this week, I'm tired.*

Of course, Tracey had tried to get Brian to hold a conversation with her. He'd refused to do more than be courteous. Of all the responses she could have received to her pregnancy news, she wasn't prepared to hear him speak something so vicious.

Are you sure it's mine?

His comment had wounded her. The words rang in her ears, vibrated in her brain, hit her nerves, and kept resonating.

Are you sure it's mine? Mine? Mine? Mine?

The answer was simple.

Yes. Who else's baby could it be? Tracey wasn't the type of woman to smile in other men's faces behind her husband's back. Yes, she'd texted Kyle, but nothing even mildly inappropriate appeared in any of those messages. But given the flat relationship between the two men, the fact that Tracey and Kyle had communicated anything to one another and Brian didn't know about it would be enough to turn him cold.

Now he'd finally thawed out.

"Tracey? Honey?"

She kept her eyes shut. "Yes."

"I didn't mean it. It's just, those texts surprised me. They bothered me."

"I hear you."

"I'm getting up now, okay?"

"Okay."

She lay against her pillow, her body curled up in a fetal position beneath the comforter. Listening as Brian shuffled around the room, she didn't move until she heard the bedroom door open and shut.

Lord, please provide an extra dose of your grace for me today.

Today would definitely be a whispered prayer day. Every hour, Tracey would pray as she pressed her way through, because Brian's words had hurt. And even though she understood it, his silence wounded her even more. He should have responded with amazement. Should have held her, prayed with her, and drove her to the Walgreen's for a pregnancy test. When they arrived home that night, he should have undressed her slowly, pressed his strong body to hers, and loved her with fire and intensity.

What did she get instead?

She got iced out.

Tracey sat up and touched her abdomen through her nightshirt. It had been eight years since she'd thought about a baby growing inside.

The body changes were enough to tell her she was carrying another kid. There had only been two other times in her life when, every day, she woke up a little nauseous, stayed hungry all day long, and went to sleep exhausted every night. That first time, Tyler was on the way. The second time was with Brianna. When she noticed the pattern two few weeks earlier, she figured it was a fluke. That was, until she scrolled backwards on her phone calendar and saw she'd missed her cycle in March. She hadn't taken a pregnancy test though. She'd wanted to talk it over with Brian and take it with him in the room.

Brushing her teeth and taking a shower would help to drive away the icky feeling. Tracey climbed out of the bed and made a beeline to the bathroom.

A new baby, in her forties and totally unplanned? Just when Brianna was old enough for Tracey to start viewing the next forty years of her life in a different way. In three years her daughter would be in middle school. Tracey had planned to start a new career when Brianna entered her pre-teen years. With a newborn, she'd have to set the clock backward another twelve years. She'd be nearly fifty-three by the time kid number three entered adolescence. Tracey had friends who retired from their jobs in their fifties.

As she turned on the shower, she shook her head as if that would bring clarity. "Lord, you are my shepherd. See me through."

❧

"Hey bestie, when are you getting back here?"

Tracey chatted on her mobile to Monica while she escorted Brianna to the field for springtime softball clinic.

"Next month," Monica answered.

"Aren't you tired of Seattle?"

"I don't know. It's nice here."

"Raining?"

"Not every day."

Tracey put her sweatshirt down on the metal bleachers, then took a seat. On the field, girls lined up to start practice. "I have news for you. I might be pregnant again."

"That's news? I thought you were going to tell me something like you all sold your house and are moving to Africa for missionary work."

"How is being pregnant not news? I'm forty."

"So what? Janet Jackson just had a son at fifty."

"Fifty?"

"Yeah. She's fine. The kid is fine. I read the story in People magazine at the airport. The chick looks giddier than when she was singing Rhythm Nation."

Tracey laughed. "I'm not all that giddy about it, but what God puts in my path is His choice. Just wish Brian and I were all right."

Monica's voice ratcheted up a notch. "Don't tell me I need to come back there and take off my earrings and put on some sneakers."

"No, nothing like that. Brian's cool." Tracey swallowed. "I told him about the pregnancy, and I just expected him to be excited about it."

"He's not?"

"No."

"Maybe he's too shocked right now. It's been almost a decade since you had a baby in the house. Give him some time."

"Yeah, but…"

Tracey stopped. Did she really want to discuss Kyle and the texts? And whether or not Tracey had been to blame. Why bother Monica with all that drama? When it all became water under the bridge, which it would, Tracey would kick herself for dragging her best friend into a bunch of relationship mess again.

"You know what, it will be all right. Brian and I will be fine. We always are."

"You both are better than fine, that's how you got pregnant again, you know."

"Yeah." She sighed. "I know."

❧

. . .

Tracey still battled her emotions as she perched in a corner of a sectional couch that Friday. The couch belonged to Kim Chase, who hosted the Friday Night House Fellowship. All married Christian women and tables full of pot luck food. Tracey had contributed a pasta salad and two bottles of ginger ale, then she sat down and ate way too much of Kim's chicken fajitas and rice. Two platefuls in fact. Her food intake? Definitely on the uptick.

She gazed around the room. All around her, there were women she could talk and laugh with, but tonight she only wanted to sit back and listen.

Toward the end of dinner hour, Kim called out to them. "Ladies, bring your dessert plates in here and find a place to sit. We need to get started."

Tracey made room on the couch for three other women to crowd in. Every chair, sofa, and floor cushion had a woman sitting on it. Eighteen ladies in total. Probably all just like Tracey. Needing prayer for their family issues or maybe even health issues. God bless Kim for starting this fellowship. Even though the Jones family attended Rise Church faithfully, and hosted life group twice a month, Tracey appreciated being able to ask for prayer on some things while away from her husband's eyes.

Kim, a Philadelphia police officer with a husky voice and warm smile, gestured toward the kitchen. "Destiny, can you turn off that light, thanks so much." She turned back to the sitting women. "Mariah? Can you open us up in a word of prayer please?"

Mariah Rodriguez, a stunning woman with a head full of dark curly hair, bowed her head. "Let us go before the throne of grace. Father, allow us to come before you in worship and with our requests. Please bless our hearts and our thoughts and our cares for one another. Allow us to be open and transparent. Speak to us, Lord, through the spirit and through your love. In Jesus' name. Amen."

When they raised their heads, Gwen Bryland, one of Rise Church's soloists, started to sing, her soft soprano filling the room with sound. Holy, holy, holy, Lord God almighty. Some of the women joined in.

Others simply listened, allowing themselves to remain still in worship. Gwen finished, and after a moment of silence, women started raising their hands in the air. One by one, they asked for prayer. Every prayer request would be recognized. Nothing too large or too small.

Tracey didn't raise her hand right away. She wanted to pray for the others first, but by the time an hour passed, she was ready to ask for prayer. Should she make it an unspoken? No. Kim encouraged them to be transparent. Tracey raised her hand.

Kim smiled. "Mrs. Tracey Jones has the floor."

"Ladies," Tracey sighed. "It has been an interesting week for me." She cleared her throat. "I believe I am pregnant."

Sounds of awww and congratulations mommy filled the room. She nodded and allowed the noise to die down before she continued. "Thanks everyone, but my prayer request tonight is for my marriage. It's a very long story as to why, but I need your prayers for me and for Brian, and for this new child."

Kim caught her eye. "Are you worried about him wanting this child?"

"Not at all." Tracey sat up straighter. "It's just complicated, that's all."

"Everyone let's pray over Tracey. I'll start," Kim said.

❧

After fellowship ended, Kim caught up with Tracey as she walked toward her car.

"Mrs. Jones," Kim clucked her tongue. "Your eyes said you wanted to talk more, but you hesitated tonight."

Tracey stopped moving. "I know. You read me right."

"You want to talk about it now?"

She might as well get it of her chest. At least she'd have someone who could pray more specifically. "Last week, Brian found a bunch of texts on my phone between me and Kyle. My son's father. Remember me talking about him?"

Kim nodded. "Uh huh. Go on."

"His father is dying from Parkinson's and he's having a hard time. I've been sending him scripture and encouragement texts to help him out. But see, Brian and I made an agreement that neither of us is supposed to secretly communicate with someone of the opposite sex. So, Brian was mad for a couple of days and he had the nerve to ask me if this was his child. He's doing better now, but I know he was hurt."

"Oh, I could see that. I'd be ticked at your behind too, baby or no baby."

"Kim!"

"Tracey, you know stuff like that drives husbands crazy. If Jesse found some mess like that in my phone, you'd still hear him yelling. Wives, we'd be seething a little, but eventually we'd concentrate on the content of the messages. Hubbies don't see content. Hubbies see another man texting their wives and they want to kill someone."

Tracey sighed. "All right. I get it. What should I do?"

"Apologize about the messages."

"I did that already."

"Then stay in prayer for hubby. He's probably more scared than anything. Help him feel secure."

❧

That Sunday, Tracey stood in the hallway at Rise, right outside of room 301. It was after four PM and Brian's Health & Wellness ministry meeting should be over. After church, Tracey drove Brianna over to stay with Ricky, Charla, and little Ricky for the rest of the afternoon and evening. Then she rushed home, showered and changed, pulled together some clothing and personal items for them, and headed back to church.

She waited as the room emptied, nodding her hellos to the ministry members who exited. When she was sure only Brian remained, she strolled into the room.

Brian stood by the desk in the front of the room, closing the bag that held his files and papers for the ministry. "Tracey?"

"Yeah…um…" She moved forward until she stood only a few feet away from him. "Tonight, I don't want to cook dinner, do laundry, get ready for the week, or do any of that. I don't even want to watch my daughter, so I took her to her aunt and uncle."

He raised an eyebrow. "Oh really?"

She stepped closer. "Really. You know what I want?"

"What?"

"I want to be with you." She took another step, this time so close she could reach out and grab him. "I'm kidnapping you and taking you away and I'm not releasing you until you understand I'm your wife and I love you and I'm not going anywhere. I know why you've been cold, but if you keep being mean to me, you're going to look crazy, because this woman right here only wants you."

Brian dropped his chin to his chest and a small chuckle escaped.

Tracey took another step. This time she was so close she could kiss him. "I am in your face right now, the car keys are in my hand, and brother, you are coming with me. Mother of your daughter and your new son or daughter. Are you going to shut me out?"

He released his bag and it fell to the desk as he put his arms around her. "I can't shut you out. I love you too much."

"You better come on then. We've got lost time to make up for."

❧

That Tuesday, another text arrived on Tracey's phone from Kyle. She spied the message on her screen as she picked up Brianna from school. He'd texted, *Today isn't a good day for my father. I'm not having a great week.*

She didn't respond right away. Instead, she waited until they reached the house. When her daughter went to her room to change clothes, she texted him back. *I'm sorry about that. I promise to stay in prayer for your entire family, but let me be clear about this, I won't be texting you anymore. Please don't text me again.*

When she read the message back to herself, it seemed harsh. Was she wrong to have texted Kyle to begin with? Well, maybe or maybe not. But Tracey adored Brian and they'd come too far to allow tension to rise between them now. Whether or not she was wrong for sending those encouragement messages, she would not contact Kyle again.

Period.

THE MARRIAGE RETREAT WEEKEND. It had to have happened there.

"Hon, how many times are you gonna pee? You want some more water to drink?" Brian joked from outside the bathroom door. "I can drive back to Walgreens and buy more tests."

"I just want to be sure."

"Three tests?"

"That stupid retreat!"

"What?"

Tracey zipped up her jeans and opened the bathroom door. She waved him in and stood back with her arms crossed. On the edge of the sink lay three EPT sticks with plus signs showing in the middle of them. He peered at the results.

Positive. Positive. And...positive.

He sat down on the edge of the tub, still staring at the pregnancy tests. "Wow. Okay. We have a new baby coming." A smile spread across his face as he looked over at his wife.

Tracey kept her arms crossed. "How is this possible?"

Brian gave a small shrug like he didn't know, then he rubbed his jaw and nodded. "Timing I guess. And that marriage retreat."

"That's what I was thinking."

Like she'd figured, the married couples retreat had something to do with it. Tracey had been determined to go because most of their married friends were going, and the planned activities promised a great time. Besides the events, Tracey and Brian had enjoyed one another passionately all weekend long.

"So, this is your fault?" She said with a smile.

He shrugged. "I'll take that, I can accept it. Baby on the way. It's official." He stood up, opening his arms wide. "Come on honey, let's get some breakfast. I know you're probably hungry."

She walked into his arms, enjoying his embrace. "I'm starving. How did you guess?"

"You were the same way with Brianna. Now with this little guy you have growing, I think you'll eat us out of house and home."

They walked out of the bathroom together and Tracey reached out and pinched Brian's arm. "How do you know it's a boy?"

Brian grinned. "I have a daughter and I love my daughter. This time when I went to buy those pregnancy tests, I sat in the car and prayed for a son. I believe God is going to answer my prayers."

"God already answered your prayers, you've had a son for years."

"I love Tyler with all my heart, but you know as well as I do, Ty is really Kyle's son."

Tracey stopped before she opened their bedroom door. "That's really how you see it?"

He reached past her and pulled the door open. "That's how it is. But I accepted that a long time ago, back when he was ten and he told me he'd never ever call me Dad because he had a real dad, and his dad's name was Kyle."

Tracey turned Brian's statement over and over in her mind as they walked down to the kitchen together. Tyler actually said that? He had always called Brian by his first name, but Tracey figured that was something they worked out together out of respect for Kyle. She never imagined young Tyler would sound so disrespectful to the man who helped raise him.

She watched as Brian put coffee in the machine and pressed the brew button. "I never knew," she said.

"Knew what?"

"Tyler said that to you. About the dad thing?"

Brian pulled their red mugs out of the cupboard. "I figured you didn't, but it was one of those things, you know. It made it a challenge to love him unconditionally, but in the end, it never stopped me from treating him like I was his biological father. In his high school years, Ty kind of shut me out, but that was for a bunch of different reasons. I'd hurt his mom and, you know, things got messy."

"Brian, I'm sorry about that."

"You don't have to apologize for something you had no control over." He poured steaming black liquid into the mugs and brought them over to the kitchen island. "I've always wanted another child, and I'd like to have a son, so maybe this is God's way of providing a blessing. It's now or never."

She reached to put sugar in her mug, but then Brian blocked her hand and took the coffee away.

"Hey! I wanted that."

"Hey, newly pregnant woman, no coffee for you, baby boy Jones doesn't need the stimulants." Brian told her. "Didn't mean to tease you, but now I'm thinking clearly. Good pregnancy health starts today."

Baby boy Jones?

Hmm. Maybe?

CHAPTER
Four

IF THE PINK pregnancy test lines she saw a month earlier weren't enough to convince Tracey she would be a mother again, the warm jelly her OB/GYN spread across her lower abdomen certainly did. Brian stood next to her, holding her hand, and together they studied the white and gray images on the monitor.

Dr. Bruce McCallum slid the fetal ultrasound wand across her gelled skin. "Yes, yes. Congratulations are in definitely in order. Dr. and Mrs. Jones, there's your baby resting in the sac right there."

On the examination table, Tracey strained to get a good look at the screen. At only a few weeks, the sac looked like nothing more than a little round blob. "There's my little guy or girl. Can't get any more official than this."

"It's early, but I think I can detect this for you. Hold on." Dr. McCallum applied more pressure to her abdomen, then touched the screen and the sound of galloping horses filled the room.

"Heartbeat! Yes, there it is!" Brian squeezed her hand. "Sounds good and strong and healthy."

"Healthy is definitely what we want." Dr. McCallum moved the doppler around Tracey's belly again. "The position looks good, and from the size..." He tapped the keyboard several times. "This is a nearly nine-week-old fetus."

Tracey looked up at Brian. An age and a heartbeat. A baby. Their new baby.

Dr. McCallum took the ultrasound away and passed Tracey a wad of tissue. She wiped the gel away from her belly, pulled up the waistband of her underwear and let Brian help her sit up on the examination table.

"Physically, everything looks good so far," Dr. McCallum said. "After you get dressed, come on in my office and we'll talk over a few things."

❦

Before Tracey sat in the chair in Dr. McCallum's office, she braced herself. This would be the 'older moms' talk. Brian had mentioned it when they drove over to the office. He told her not to become anxious, but the doctor would talk about her maternal age and all the risks involved with giving birth in her forties.

Dr. McCallum sat back in his office chair. "Your blood pressure, weight, and all your vitals are great, I want to let you know that first."

"Okay," Tracey said.

"But I need to discuss a few other issues with you, particularly because of your and Dr. Jones ages."

She glanced at Brian. "Dr. Jones age?"

Dr. McCallum continued. "Yes, Dr. Jones, you're how old now?"

"I'm forty-four."

"I'm asking because research has found that while maternal age isn't a factor, advanced paternal age does show an increase in the like-lihood of autism."

Tracey dug her nails into the fabric on the chair arms. "Do we know how much of an increase?"

"Now that depends on a few factors. While the research isn't conclusive yet, we do know the increase is higher with family history. But unlike other chromosomal abnormalities, we don't have a way to test for autism. For Down Syndrome or other issues, I'll recommend you for non-invasive prenatal screening, where your blood is screened without any risk to your baby."

Tracey looked over at her husband. His face hadn't changed a bit. He looked happy on the way to the office, he was over the moon during the ultrasound, and he appeared completely relaxed as he listened to Dr. McCallum.

"These are all things I need you to know, but please don't obsess over them. The risks are only slightly higher, and they are risks, not predictions." Dr. McCallum added, looking at Tracey. "You recently turned forty?"

Tracey nodded.

"Since you're over thirty-five, your risks for certain pregnancy issues are a little higher. Gestational diabetes and pre-eclampsia are two big issues, but we'll keep monitoring your blood sugar and blood pressure throughout the pregnancy. Placenta issues could occur, and we'll keep a close eye on that as well. Miscarriage is likely your biggest risk."

She listened without comment. For all these things Dr. McCallum mentioned, there wasn't much she could do except stay healthy and stay in prayer.

Brian reached over for Tracey's hand. "Doctor, do you see the look on my wife's face. Can you please give her something good to think on? Something that can bring down her stress hormones?"

Dr. McCallum glanced at her file. "You got it. Mrs. Jones, you are in terrific health. You aren't on any medications, and you are the right weight for your height. And for all the risks I mentioned, those are statistics for the general population. Plenty of women your age and older give birth to healthy children. Oh, and here's some real good news for you, mothers over age forty tend to be better moms."

"Thanks," Tracey said, gazing down at the carpet. "I'll keep all that in mind."

In the car, Brian put the keys in the ignition. "How are you doing?"

Tracey shrugged. "Fine, I guess." She put on her safety belt, then reclined the passenger seat. "It's hard to listen to all those risks and then put on a happy face. We didn't plan any of this."

"Well, I am happy, whether it was planned or unplanned." He backed out of the parking space, then directed the car toward the lot exit. "Not everything good is planned, and our God works through all things."

"I know."

"You're still nervous though. I know you're over there digging your nails into the car seat."

Tracey sighed. "Downs Syndrome. Autism. Miscarriage risks. None of that bugs you?"

"I see it this way, the Lord will give us the child he wants us to have. You don't have a history of miscarriages, so I'm not worried about that. I trust Him."

"I trust Him too, I just—"

"What?"

"It's a lot to think about."

Of course, their new baby growing inside of her filled her with a certain amount of joy. But would she carry it to term? What if she miscarried? Or, what if she carried to term, but the baby had issues like Down Syndrome? Or, the baby could be fine initially, but then have developmental delays or autism detected at a later date.

Continuing with the pregnancy would mean accepting all the risks. But really, what could she do? Abortion was out of the question for them, even if the prenatal screening showed chromosomal issues. But the Lord knew about their advanced ages. And forty wasn't that old, was it? Tracey's Aunt Zee had given birth to her last child at the age of forty-two. That child, Tracey's younger cousin, Lynn, grew up to be one the smartest members of her family, having earned a degree in particle physics from UC Berkeley.

She glanced over at Brian. Still ecstatic. Compared to the look on his face the night at Talula's Garden when he found those texts from Kyle on her phone, today was a massive improvement. Since they'd made up about that issue, he hadn't mentioned a word about it. He probably hadn't forgotten, but the reality of baby Jones on the way had pretty much taken over.

Thank God their marriage was on strong footing. Everything in the past would stay in the past. She learned her lesson with the texting and that was all water under the bridge.

Nothing could touch their union now.

TYLER SPORTED A THICKER goatee and too much hair on his head, but Tracey was still happy to see him on FaceTime.

"Good to hear from you." Tracey rested her phone against the kitchen windowsill, so she could talk to her son while she cleaned. "It's been a minute."

"Been spending all my extra time around Grandma and Grandpop. Plus, classes are tougher this semester. I've been studying then collapsing afterward."

She used a sponge to scrub the sink. "Ready to choose a major yet?"

"Yeah, it's going to be accounting. I have my sights on one of those big firm jobs after graduation."

"As long as it's a field you're interested in. Don't choose something because you think it's safe or it will make you a lot of money."

"Then it's okay if I change my major to Poetry?"

"Ty?"

He started cracking up. "Come on Mom, I'm just kidding."

"Good." She stopped moving and looked at the phone screen. "Um…I've got some news to share with you."

"What?"

"I'm about nine weeks pregnant. I've having another child."

Tracey watched as Tyler's face went slack. "You're joking right? You're saying that because I made a joke about a Poetry major?"

"No son, I'm not."

"So, you serious?"

"Yes, I am." She stepped back and pointed to her abdomen. "I'm not showing yet, but I will in a few months. Before you ask, my health is fine, and I feel good so far."

"Wow, mom. I don't know what to say."

"Uh, congratulations would be good."

"I mean, if this is what you want, it's cool, I guess. But I'm thinking—"

"What?"

"I'm just saying, I'm about to start my second year in college soon. You really want to go back to taking care of a baby? Shouldn't you be looking forward to your grandchildren now."

Tracey raised her eyebrows. "You having kids anytime soon?"

"No."

"Well, then, it's not time for grandchildren and your new brother or sister is on the way," she said. "And it would be good if you sent some well wishes Brian's way."

"Yeah, all right." His eyes shifted downward.

Time to nip this in the bud. Tracey loved them both. She could pray for their relationship, but it was high time they tried to meet each other halfway.

"Tyler, I've said this before and I'm saying it again, I know you've got a bromance going on with your own dad, but Brian is the one who put a roof over your head, mentored you, prayed for you, and kept you eating and drinking from the time you were in elementary school 'til you walked out of this house for Hofstra."

"I know."

"Yeah, I know you know, but you need to be a little more grateful to him." She lowered her voice. "Holding a grudge against him because of some allegiance you have to your father, or even because you hate what Brian did one time in our relationship, that's dumb. If I'm doing fine, which I am, you need to forgive and forget."

"Mom, we're good, okay."

"That's fine, Ty, I just want you to act like it."

Tracey bit her tongue to keep from saying more. Tyler adored Kyle. Wonderful. Awesome. A son should love his dad. But Tracey had never told him the full story of his conception and the nine months when she was pregnant. How Kyle tried to force her have an abortion, then broke up with her when she wouldn't. She'd never shared about those long lonely days when she moved back to Philly and lived with her aunt and uncle until she gave birth, and how she was only able to communicate with Kyle's parents, the Addisons. Eventually Kyle came around, accepting his role as father and building a strong relationship with Tyler from the time he was two onward. But those first years? Tracey had been alone.

"Anything else going on?" Tyler asked.

"Not much," Tracey said as she sprinkled more cleanser into the stainless steel sink. "Your little sister is growing bigger each day. She misses you. You need to call her too."

"How's she doing at softball?"

"Terrible. But she likes it."

"Tell her I'm gonna call her on Friday night, okay. Maybe she can come up and visit soon?"

"She keeps thinking you'll come back here. It's not like we put you out permanently when you left for college."

"I haven't had the time. With my classes and with Grandpop not doing well, I get scared that if I travel down there, he'll pass away and I won't have the chance to say goodbye. Dad feels the same way. I don't think he's traveled anywhere far since Grandpop started getting round the clock nursing."

"Ty, tell him I'm praying for him, and for your grandfather. I...just tell him I'm keeping them all in prayer."

"No problem. Mom, I gotta go. I have to go to work in an hour and I still need to finish typing stuff for a paper."

"Fine. Love you."

"Love you too."

Tracey wiped her hands with a paper towel then pressed the button to end the call on her phone. Kyle staying close to home, huh? He must be scared. That didn't mean she had to call him. It only meant she needed to keep the whole Addison family in prayer. It could be days or weeks before Judge Thaddeus Addison passed.

She finished cleaning the kitchen and moved on to the family room when her phone buzzed again. She picked it up and looked at the Caller ID. A broad smile creased her face as she pressed the button to answer.

"Sis!"

"Hey preggo!" Charla Jones, Tracey's sister-in-law, spoke with joy in her voice. "Congratulations and bless you for giving little Ricky a childhood playmate. Good looking out. Knew I could count on ya."

Tracey laughed. "You better thank God because you know this wasn't planned at all."

"Doesn't matter. You have two other kids. You know what to do. Think Brian might get that boy? Ricky said he hasn't seen his brother this excited since the day he got married."

"I know. That man is on top of the world right now."

"And I thought y'all were two and done."

Tracey eased down on the family room couch. "Me, too. I came with one son, then we had our daughter, and we had one talk over the years about having another kid. But that was right before we started having marriage issues, and he never brought it up again after that." She yawned. "He keeps saying he wants a boy, but honestly, I just want everything to go well. It's the health stuff that scares me."

"Your doctor gave you the scary pregnancy speech?"

"He sure did."

"Sis, don't sweat it, you know that's what they have to do. Saves them from malpractice."

"We still haven't told Brianna yet. I told Tyler today, though."

"How is my college nephew?"

"Busy as ever. He didn't sound too happy to find out he'll be twenty with a new brother or sister, but I think it just surprised him."

"Well, over here in this house, we're happy for you all. Whenever you're ready, let's go out to dinner to celebrate. Text me a day and time and I'll coordinate with Ricky, all right."

"Sounds good. Thanks Charla."

With Tyler knowing about the pregnancy, Tracey figured she should scheme a way to tell Brianna.

The girl could not resist a surprise. That day, before Tracey picked her up from school, she stopped by the Family Dollar and purchased a small plastic baby doll wrapped in a fleece baby blanket. She also bought some multicolored art markers and a sketch book. Before Brianna started her homework, Tracey would present them to her.

In the house, Brianna dropped her purple backpack on the floor and made a beeline for the pantry.

Tracey stopped her. "What are you doing?"

"Can I make chocolate milk?"

"As soon as you wash your hands and face and change out of your uniform."

"But I'm thirsty."

Tracey pointed to the staircase. "Go. It won't take you but a few minutes. When you come back, you can have your milk."

Brianna frowned, but she still turned and obeyed her mother's commands.

Good. With Brianna upstairs changing, Tracey could set everything up. As soon as she heard Brianna's feet climbing the stairs, she dashed back to the car and retrieved the Family Dollar bag from the trunk. In the kitchen, she pulled out the baby doll and the markers and sketch book and lined them all up on the kitchen island.

Changed into a gray zip-up sweat suit, Brianna padded back into the kitchen. She must have pulled her uniform off in a rush because some of her hair stuck out of the ballet bun on top of her head. A questioning look crossed her face when she stared at the kitchen island.

"Mom? Whose toys?"

Tracey sat on a stool. "Come on over and sit here, and those aren't toys."

Brianna climbed up on a stool. "This is a doll baby."

"I know."

"Why'd you give me a doll baby?"

Tracey pointed to the doll. "This is not just a doll, Brianna. This is a symbol. It represents something."

"What?" Brianna asked, her eyebrows furrowed.

"You don't want to guess?"

"No."

Tracey rolled her eyes. "Mommy is pregnant. I'm going to have a baby."

Brianna's eyes grew wide. "I'm going to have a sister!"

"Or a brother. Whatever God gives us." Tracey smiled. "Are you happy?"

She grinned wide, showing that her side teeth were missing. "A new baby. I don't have to sleep in a room with it, do I? Because babies cry and stink."

"No, Bri, the baby will have a nursery."

"Then I'm happy." Brianna slid down off the stool, came over and wrapped her arms around Tracey's waist. "It will be cute, and I'll help you take care of it, okay. Does Daddy know?"

"Of course he knows." Tracey pointed to the sketch book. "I want you to use the markers and book to draw pictures for the baby's room, okay. You have an important job, welcoming a new little person to our family and home. It's a big responsibility."

"I'll do it. I'll draw something new everyday." Brianna squeezed tighter. "Love you, mommy."

Tracey smoothed her daughter's hair. With all this love surrounding her now, if she could bottle this moment and keep it with her, she'd caress it each time worry tempted her. For right now though, she would keep holding onto her daughter and hope for the best during the pregnancy.

That night Tracey couldn't find a comfortable spot anywhere in the bed. She turned face up and she stared at the ceiling. She flipped onto her belly and the pillows bunched up in her face too much. On her side, snuggling Brian, she rested with her cheek on his shoulder and thought she might get to sleep, but then the heat from his body made her too warm and she slid away. When she turned over on her other side, Brian moved with her and put his arm and leg over her body, trapping her in that position.

Tracey sighed, staring at the glowing digits on the bedside clock. Five after one and she might have slept a total of an hour since going to bed at ten. At least she wasn't having bad dreams. Those would be the worst.

Instead, her mind worked like a pepper mill, grinding every bit of information she'd received in the past month. Forty years-old with a forty-four year-old husband and they were having a surprise pregnancy. A son who wasn't all that happy to hear that news. A doctor who warned them of Down Syndrome, autism, miscarriages, and gestational problems.

And what if she gave birth to a special needs child? Did she even possess the amount of love and care she would need to care for the child properly? She'd always looked up to women who championed their differently abled children. She even admired Lisette Santana for that, of all people. Last year, Lisette moved with her son Elijah, who possessed a mild form of cerebral palsy, to Loma Linda, California so she could raise him in one of the healthiest areas in America. That took real mommy warrior guts.

News of the baby seemed to displace every plan Tracey had considered for the upcoming eighteen years. Her own desires seemed to shrink, folding down into her mind so small she hadn't bothered to pull them out to voice them. What about the part of her content with the routine she, Brian, and Brianna had in the household right now? And how about her dreams of having a career after her daughter entered middle school?

Her feelings? A mixed bag at best. Joyful, but cautious. Loving, but worried. Excited, but resentful. Sure, she'd accepted God's will for her life, but she'd be lying to herself if she insisted all her emotions were good ones.

Brian's sleepy voice broke through the quiet. "Trace? You okay."

"I'm fine."

"I can feel you. You keep moving around."

"I might need to get something to eat. I'm having a hard time falling asleep."

He rubbed her belly through her nightgown. "You want me to go make you some soup or a sandwich?"

She put her hand over his and closed her eyes. "No, what I really want to do is get to sleep and stop thinking so much."

"Thinking about the baby?"

"Yes." And other things.

"Honey, it's going to be okay, I promise. Don't stress yourself or lose sleep. Let's pray about it."

"Brian—"

"Come on now, if it's worth thinking about, it's worth praying about, so I need to cover you with prayer right now."

She remained still as he wrapped his arms around her and prayed.

"Heavenly Father, my wife is worried right now, and she needs you. We love this child and we accept your will for our lives, but we cannot see the future. Please give us the wisdom to know what to do in the situations you lead us to and provide us with the courage and strength to handle what comes before us. We love you, Lord. Amen."

After prayer, some of Tracey's tension began to melt away. She moved deeper into Brian's embrace and drifted to sleep.

❧

Two hours later, Tracey woke again. Pushing Brian's arms away from her body, she sat up and swung her legs over the side of the bed. Maybe she should have gotten something to eat after all? She'd go right to the kitchen after she went to the bathroom. She'd almost forgotten that being pregnant meant she'd pee a lot more often.

In their bathroom, she shut the door. The robin's egg blue night light plugged into the wall provided enough illumination to help her see her way to the toilet. She pulled down her underwear and sat down.

What was that? She peered closer at the cotton crotch of her panties. Three different sized dark dots. Hot electricity darted through her body as she lunged up and flipped the light switch fast.

Three large brick colored dots.

She peered closer.

Blood?

On the toilet, she stayed immobilized, breathing in and out. Her heart beat fast and she began to sweat.

All those negative, selfish thoughts. Mourning the loss of her free time, thinking about the burden on her, doubting her ability to care for a child different than the ones she already had.

Could God be so fed up that he made her decision for her?

CHAPTER

Six

DR. MCCALLUM MOVED the fetal ultrasound wand around Tracey's lower belly for a few moments, then he spoke the words that put her fears to rest. "Your baby is just fine. I don't see any issues here."

Tracey breathed a sigh of relief. *Thank you, Lord, and please forget all those selfish thoughts I had.*

"Want to hear the heartbeat before you leave?"

She nodded. "Yes, please."

The doctor pressed against her abdomen one more time, and just like her visit before, she heard the sound of galloping horses. A nice strong heartbeat at ten weeks.

"If I'm not having a miscarriage, where's the bleeding coming from?" Tracey asked.

He pulled the wand away. "Don't think of it as bleeding. Actual pregnancy bleeding flows like your cycle, and it usually indicates a miscarriage. What you're experiencing is spotting, and that can happen throughout your first trimester as your placenta grows and the baby implants."

"I feel so silly." Tracey wiped her lower belly with a paper towel as she sat up. "I told my husband about it this morning, and he told me it was only implantation spotting. But I couldn't rest until I knew for sure."

Dr. McCallum chuckled. "Don't feel silly. We want our patients to be cautious. If you think it's an emergency, we do everything we can to get you in here."

"Well, I appreciate it."

"Is everything else going well? Having any trouble with morning sickness, or any pain?"

"No, not at all." Tracey watched as the doctor turned off the ultrasound monitor. "I'm hungry all the time, but that's it."

"Eat whenever you feel like it, keep your nutrition high, and keep taking your vitamins. We'll see you next month, okay Mrs. Jones?"

"See you then."

As soon as the door shut, Tracey slid down from the table, got her purse from the chair where she left it and pulled out her phone. She called Brian and left a voice mail. Her phone rang right after she left the office, as soon as she crossed the parking lot.

"Hey honey," she answered.

"How did it go?"

"Good. No problems. Nothing to be concerned about."

"Implantation spotting?"

Tracey opened the car door and put her purse inside before climbing in. "You were right, okay. You were right."

She heard Brian snort. "I'm a doctor and you don't trust me. I should be offended."

Tracey sighed. "Cut me some slack. I've never had a miscarriage, I don't know what it looks like. I saw red spots and I freaked out."

"But you're relaxed now?"

"Yes." She rested her back on the seat. "Dr. McCallum said the baby is fine. The heartbeat sounds strong and—"

Tracey's phone vibrated in her hand. She looked at the screen. Tyler?

"Honey, I'm getting a call from Tyler. Call you back later?"

"Sure, talk to you later," Brian said.

She tapped to switch to Tyler's call.

He sounded flustered. "Mom?"

"Yes."

"I have class all day morning, then I have work this afternoon. But they're moving Grandpop today. They're moving him from the house."

Tracey dropped her keys to her lap. "Moving him where?"

"To the hospital. Grandma told me he's having a rough time swallowing, and his doctor is concerned he might have an infection. Mom, he's going and I won't be able to say goodbye to him. I think I need to skip my classes today."

"Tyler listen, they're probably moving him to care for him better. Did your grandmother actually tell you she thought he was going to pass away?"

"No."

"Then you need to stay calm and wait for more news. In the meantime, finish your classes and keep in touch with your family in between. When your grandpop gets to the hospital, they'll make him comfortable and you'll get to see him tonight."

"You sure?"

"I'm positive. Remember when my dad had his stroke and you wanted to leave New York and come back down here?"

"Yeah."

"Where's your other grandfather now?"

"At home."

"Right. So think about that. Just because a loved one goes to the hospital doesn't mean they will stay there."

"But mom, seriously, he's not doing too good now. Me, Dad, Grandma, no one's been saying it, but this might be it."

Tracey looked through the windshield. Cars moved around, searching for parking spots. And here she was trying to find a way to keep things positive on the phone with Tyler. This was a challenge. Judge Addison had been ailing with Parkinson's for years, and he was in stage five now. She didn't want to alarm her son, but his fears might not be unfounded.

"Son, please pray and understand that all things are under God's control."

"Go to class?"

"Go to class. And you can call me later if you need, okay. I'm always here."

She heard him take a breath and let it out. "Mom give Grandma a call. She said she hasn't heard from you in a long time."

"I will."

Tyler ended the call, but Tracey still sat with the phone in her hand. Tyler's heart had to be breaking. His beloved grandfather, the one who planted kisses all over his face the day after his birth, would probably leave this earth soon. Ms. Celeste, who'd been strong all those years by her husband's side, must be grieving already. And Kyle? Tracey didn't even want to think about it. He had to be mourning too.

Tracey started the car and looked in the rearview mirror. At first, she scanned the area behind her to make sure no other cars were coming, then she leaned up further and stared at her reflection. A mother with two children and one on the way, and two families she loved. Her responsibilities were to Brian and their household, but that didn't erase the concern in her heart for the Addison family. Especially for Judge Addison. If not for his generosity, Tracey and Tyler would have been homeless the year he was born. Then later, when she escaped to their home after that huge fight with Brian, they allowed her to stay there with no questions asked. She had to call Ms. Celeste and pray with her. And she should probably say something to Kyle, but if Brian even thought she wanted to do that, all peace in the Jones household would cease.

She backed out of the space, then shifted gears and drove forward.

Tracey, who are you? Where do your loyalties lie?

THE LIVING ROOM held a seat for everyone. Food for their Tuesday evening life group session was spread out on a buffet in the dining room. Baked mushroom chicken, wild rice, green salad and buttered rolls. The hard part would be convincing Brian and Brianna not to eat any of it. Tracey had pulled together a surprise for them after life group ended, and she didn't want them spoiling their appetites.

The Jones' used their Chestnut Hill home to host twice monthly life group sessions for the last two years. At each session, ten or so members of Rise Church would arrive for a light meal, Bible study, worship, and prayer. Sometimes other families provided the food, but tonight it was the Joneses turn to cook for the others.

A few minutes before seven, Brian chased Brianna downstairs and they headed straight toward the dining room. Tracey stretched her arms and legs out to physically block their way at the doorway.

"Stop," she announced. "None for you tonight! Just pour yourself some iced tea and go on into the living room."

"Mom! Come on!"

"Tracey, what're you doing?" Brian chuckled.

She pointed toward the living room. "Now all the food in this room is for the life group, but I have something very special for both of you after the session is over and I want you to save your appetites. Go on, make yourselves comfortable in the living room and be patient."

"But I'm huuunngrrry." Brianna marched around in a circle, trying to get past her mother.

Tracey planted a kiss on her forehead, then turned her back toward the kitchen. "You'll live. Like I said, get something to drink."

Brian raised an eyebrow. "Let's do what your mom says. I don't know what she's up to, but I think it'll be good."

"Oh, it will be." She winked at him.

Right on schedule, the front door opened and for the next ten minutes, members of their life group trickled in. Jesse and Kim Chase arrived first, with their young sons, Jarvis and Kinard, trailing behind them. Next came Rev. Alex Robinson and the nephew he cared for, nine-year-old Samson. Then there was Tonya and Lance Black, and Leonard Dockens and his wife, Lisa. Bringing up the rear was Chablis Shields, a young single Christian with a sunny disposition who had recently started dating a young man named John Gerald, whom Brian mentored.

When everyone was inside and greeted everyone else, Brian, who served as life group leader, opened up in a word of prayer.

He stood in the dining room doorway. "Lord, we thank you for bringing us all together tonight. Thank you, also, for allowing us to worship you, and thank you for this food for the nourishment of our bodies. Amen."

As their life group served themselves, Tracey settled by Brian's side, her arm around his waist. He whispered down to her, "You're still not going to tell me what you have going on?"

"Nope."

"Just full of surprises this season?"

"Yup."

At nearly nine o'clock that June evening, Tracey led her husband and daughter to the back yard patio. She instructed them keep their eyes covered as they walked out the backdoor.

After they stepped onto the deck, she told them, "Okay, you can open your eyes now."

In front of her family, on the redwood picnic table, Tracey had laid out a gold table cloth and white candles in crystal holders. She'd placed their favorite meals on silver dishes with formal dining setting. For Brianna, a hot deep dish cheese pizza from Uno Pizzeria and Grill, along with sliced green apples and a caramel dipping sauce. For Brian and Tracey, prime rib and green beans almandine courtesy of their local steakhouse. Their water glasses held sparkling Pellegrino. In the middle of the table was a fresh red velvet cheesecake straight from the Cheesecake Factory. She'd had to sneak out of life group a few times to warm everything and have it ready for them, but her surprise worked.

"I wanted to take some time out to show you both how much I love you, and that I think of you all the time. Oh, and to celebrate our new little one on the way." She gestured to their spread. "These are your favorites, so please, let's enjoy our private backyard picnic here."

Brian sat down at the picnic table. "I never would have guessed. You've outdone yourself this time." He shook his head, then offered his hand to her. "Come here."

Tracey eased down next to her husband. He leaned over and kissed her cheek. "Love you."

"I love you too."

Brianna grinned, her mouth already full of pizza. "I love this! You are the best mommy ever!"

"Remember that the next time I tell you to clean your room or finish your homework."

"What's that?" Brianna pointed to the silver box next to the cheesecake.

"Don't know." Tracey shrugged. "Why don't you take a look?"

Brianna didn't skip a beat. She reached over and grabbed the box, opening the lid in one smooth movement. She moved aside tissue paper, then pulled out a Fujifilm Instax Mini 90 instant film camera.

"Whoa!" Brian's eyes grew wide. "Somebody got a camera!"

Tracey gave instructions. "Brianna, I'll teach you how to use it and then you can take pictures of all of us leading up to the baby's birth, and when we get to the hospital."

Brianna's eyes grew wide. "What if I break it?"

"You're my big girl now. Once I show you how it works, you won't break it, okay. You'll be careful with it."

"A big sister responsibility, right?"

Tracey smiled. "Yes, and I have to count on you, because Mom and Dad are going to be getting the room ready and other things, so you have to play your part. You'll take the first set of pictures to paste into the baby book."

Brian tapped her shoulder. "Don't I get anything to do?"

She turned and winked, putting her arms around him. "Oh, you've already done your part, Daddy. I think that's clear."

❧

Somehow, orchestrating the late night picnic surprise for Brian and Brianna made Wednesday morning a little easier for Tracey. She cared for them deeply, there should be no doubting that. Her loyalty stood with them one thousand percent.

So she possessed zero guilt when, two hours after driving Brianna to school, she sat on a stool in the kitchen and pulled out her cell phone to call Kyle's mother, Celeste Addison.

"Ms. Celeste, how are you doing?"

"As well as I can be, and better than I deserve, I guess." Celeste sighed. "Thinking about all the good times. All the years when things weren't like this."

This was hard. "How is Judge Addison today?"

"He's going to stay in the hospital for now. He's receiving help with his swallowing and breathing. His medical team has made him comfortable, and I'll stay by his side. There's not much I need to do while he's here."

Finding the right words in these types of situations? Difficult. The Addison's had walked with the Lord for a long time. Ms. Celeste must be leaning on her faith during this season.

"He's a fighter, Ms. Celeste," Tracey said. "We're all praying, and I know he's fighting."

"Yes, yes. He is determined to hang on and stay with us a while longer, but if he doesn't, I'll know it's his season to meet his Lord. Today though, the care he's getting is excellent, and the Lord is definitely providing for both of us. That's my testimony."

"Powerful testimony."

"Yes, indeed," Celeste said. "And I heard congratulations are in order, mommy."

Tracey smiled. "Tyler told you."

"It's been awhile since I've been around a newborn, so please don't make yourself a stranger after the baby is born. I'd love to see your whole family."

Visiting the Addison home. Tracey avoided it since the whole debacle a few years ago, even though she adored Kyle's parents. Stupid, complicated relationships. Tracey had witnessed the hardness in Brian's face that evening at Talula's Garden. He managed to say it without saying it: Kyle, Celeste, Judge Addison…that's Tyler's family, not yours. Pray for them and leave them alone. But Tracey couldn't do that. And now, with Judge Addison's time on earth possibly ending shortly, it was inevitable she'd interact with the family again. She'd have to figure out a way to get Brian on board without him thinking there was more to it.

"I would love to come see you soon," Tracey said. "How is Kyle doing, by the way?"

"Actually, he just left here a few minutes before you called. He's working with some new clients. But since we brought my husband here, Kyle has been here with me every night like clockwork. Some evenings he even comes with me to pray in the chapel."

"Kyle? In the chapel?"

Celeste gave a low chuckle. "I know. I always said it would take an act of God to get him to come to church on his own. Maybe this is it? If it is, I'll take it."

"Ms. Celeste, is there anything I can do? Special prayers?"

"I really do have everything I need, but please pray for Kyle. I've seen him trying to latch on to faith in God, but I've also seen him grow bitter. And Tyler, he's trying to hang in there with his summer courses, and I don't want all this to ruin his studies. Sometimes I walk over to their living room, and I see both of them sitting there, looking lost. But my husband loves those men, and I want them to focus on that."

Tracey swallowed at the lump in her throat. This woman would likely lose her husband soon, and her requests for prayer were for her son and grandson. Strong in her faith and selfless in her actions. *Lord, if I can mature to have one tenth of the faith this woman has, that's saying something.*

"I'll pray on those things," Tracey said. "And if you need anything else, anything at all, I'll be there for you."

"Thank you, sugar. Bless you."

SEPTEMBER

Brianna's first day of the fourth grade, and she bounced around in the backseat of Tracey's car, her curly ponytail punctuating the air as she spoke a mile a minute.

"And this year, we get to build real products with motors. There's a news broadcast I can participate in…and all the girls get to help write it…and…" Brianna chattered away, repeating every single thing her mother had read to her from the fourth-grade lower school packet she received in August.

Tracey nodded her head, half listening as she directed the car toward the academy campus.

"And you are coming with me when we go to New York. It's the statue of liberty as a field trip this year."

"Yes, Brianna, I'm definitely going." Tracey steered the car onto the school grounds. "But before all of this happens, why don't you get through the first day, all right. Come home and tell us all about it."

"Mom! My friends are on the sidewalk. Can you stop? I want to walk with them."

Tracey looked around. "But we aren't up to the building yet."

"I know, but I see Anna and Maya are walking together. Can I go with them? Please. And can I invite them to church with us this year? Or life group?"

Tracey shrugged as she pulled over toward sidewalk. "Please, get through the first day, okay? We'll talk about everything else when you come home."

"Bye, Mom!" Brianna climbed out of the car and stepped onto the walkway in an instant.

Her daughter grew bigger and further away every month of her life. This was the same girl who had screamed and plastered herself to Tracey's legs on her first day of kindergarten. Now? It wouldn't be long before she didn't want her mother to drive her to school at all. That was the cycle of life for kids: bring them into the world, raise them up, let them go.

She patted her growing midsection as she steered the car out of the campus entrance. "Don't know who you are yet, baby Jones, but I pray you'll love school just as much as your sister."

A half mile away from home, Tracey's phone buzzed and danced in the cupholder. She glanced at it quickly. Tyler on FaceTime.

She could not FaceTime and drive, so she made her way to a store parking lot, put the car in park, picked up the phone and pressed the green button for Accept.

Tyler's phone number had appeared, but when the screen lit up for FaceTime, Tracey found herself staring at the face of a cute brown-skinned girl with straight dark hair falling down past her shoulders. Tyler's girlfriend Paris.

"Ms. Tracey?"

"Hi, Paris. What's going on?"

"Ty told me get you on FaceTime. We just came back to their house from the hospital. I'll let him tell you."

The screen changed from Paris' face, to a beige living room wall, to Tyler's face. His hair looked bushier than Tracey had ever seen it. His eyes? Bloodshot. With water falling from his eyes, he spoke.

"Mom? Grandpop, he's gone now." He looked away from the screen, then back again, his voice cracking. "I said goodbye."

Tyler ducked his head down and passed the phone back to Paris. He wept hard.

Judge Thaddeus Addison. Gone.

Tracey held her phone in one hand and used the other to fish around in her bag for a Kleenex.

"Tyler, honey," She wiped her own eyes. "I'm so sorry."

More weeping and sniffling, with Paris rubbing Tyler's back and shoulders for the next few minutes.

When he started to quiet down, she spoke again. "Tyler?"

"Mom." He sniffed.

"Raise your head up, honey. Come on. Look at me. I have some-thing important to remind you."

Tyler took the phone from Paris, dabbing wetness away from his face with a handkerchief.

"You were the apple of your grandfather's eye. Remember what I told you about the day after you were born?"

Tyler nodded.

"He stopped everything he was doing to drive down and see about you. You had an outstanding grandfather, through all your schooling and sports, and every summer when you stayed on Long Island. I want you to thank God for those experiences. You had a wonderful, loving, wise, grandfather who provided for you and held you close to his heart."

Tyler nodded again as he wiped his eyes. "I'll miss him."

"We all will. But the Lord was his Savior, and I look forward to seeing him again when he won't be stiff, trembling, or in pain. It might take you some time to feel that way, and that's okay."

"My Grandpop."

"Your Grandpop was amazing. Never met anyone like him."

Tyler sniffed. "Grandma is resting now. She says family's coming soon."

The words were out of Tracey's mouth before she could pull them back. "Where's your dad?"

"Laying in his room. You want to talk to him?"

Tracey almost said, I can't. Instead, she wiped her eyes again. "When you see him, tell him I'm sorry for his loss and I'm praying for him."

❧

Early in the afternoon, Tracey lay down on her side to rest. She'd drawn the curtains to keep the bedroom dim. It would be great to have a nap before the end of Brianna's school day. Tracey had cried so much earlier in the day, she was exhausted. Later, after Brian arrived home, she would tell them both about Judge Addison passing. She also wanted to call Ms. Celeste and pray with her, but she'd do that later as well.

Curled up on the bed, she placed her palms against her abdomen. Baby Jones shifted about. Tracey and Brian opted not to find out the gender, but early in the summer they did have chromosomal testing. The results came back normal.

On the nightstand, her phone buzzed.

Tracey sighed, straining her body to look at it. Tyler again.

She picked it up and answered. "Ty."

"Hey, mom."

"You all right? Your grandma?"

"We're okay. It's Dad."

Oh no! Tracey sat up. "What's wrong?"

"He wants to talk to you."

"Wait…Ty—" Tracey protested.

Kyle's deep voice came through the phone. "Tracey?"

"Kyle." Too late to do anything about it now. She'd give her condolences and tell Brian about it later. "I'm so, so sorry about your father. We lost a wonderful man."

"We did." Kyle cleared his throat. "He was strong until the end. Right up until the end, I held his hand. He looked so peaceful afterward."

"You all loved on him, right until he met his Lord." Tears streamed down Tracey's cheeks. "That's exactly how it should be."

Kyle coughed and cleared his throat again. "Anyway, I wanted to thank you for all your prayers. The funeral is next Saturday. Tyler will send you all the information."

"Yes, that's fine. Thank you."

"But you'll probably want to arrive early on Friday, so you can have a good night's sleep before the funeral. We'd like you to sing along with the choir. Oh, and congratulations, Ty told me about the new baby."

Wait. What? "Thanks, and uh…"

"I have to go check on my mom. We're looking forward to seeing you, okay. Giving you back to Ty now."

"Kyle…listen…"

Tyler's voice intruded. "Mom don't drive up here. I don't want you to get tired. Come up on the train and I'll pick you up and drive you everywhere."

Tracey sat upright. "Ty…I'm not so sure—"

"Mom, Grandpop always asked about you. All those summers I visited, he'd mention you, until he couldn't talk well anymore. Said you were the best mother his grandson could have. You have to be here. And…I need you here."

Tracey put her hand over her eyes. In less than a day, Judge Addison had passed, she still hadn't told Brian, and now Tyler and Kyle expected her to come and help sing at the funeral.

She glanced at the clock on the nightstand. Almost two-thirty.

"Ty, I have to get some rest. I'll call you later."

"Bye Mom."

By six-thirty she needed to figure out what to say on two levels. First, she'd have to explain how she just *happened* to talk to Kyle on the phone. And second, she'd have to discuss why she needed to attend Judge Addison's funeral. She sighed as she lay back down on the comforter.

Lord, this is not complicated at all. I just have to be transparent. Help me, please.

CHAPTER
Nine

IN THE HOUSE, Tracey peered out of Tyler's old bedroom window and down into the driveway. Brian hadn't arrived yet.

"Mommy," Brianna's voice echoed in the empty room.

Tracey turned around. "Yeah."

"I'm done with reading time. Can I turn on the PlayStation?"

Normally, the answer would be resounding no, but Tracey didn't have the patience to try to engage Brianna that afternoon.

"Fine. But when dinnertime comes, game time is over."

"Okay."

Tracey returned to the window. Now she stared at the top of Brian's car.

Anxiety trickled through her bloodstream. Why? She definitely wasn't afraid of her husband. But did she want to avoid having this particular conversation?

Yes.

Still, when she heard him walk into their bedroom, she exited Tyler's room and headed down the hallway.

"Hey honey," Brian sat on the bench in front of their bed, removing his black dress shoes. "You told Brianna she could play video games?"

"She finished her homework early, and I'm a little tired right now. I don't have the strength to chase her around."

"You nap today?"

"A little." She settled down beside him. "I have some bad news."

Brian stopped moving. "What?"

"Judge Addison passed away this morning."

"Oh, no. I'm really sorry to hear that. Tyler called you?"

"Yeah. I was on FaceTime with him after he left the hospital."

"How's he doing?"

"He's grieving, and he will be for a while." Tracey paused, then continued. "I talked to Kyle, too."

"Really?"

She focused her gaze on the dresser across from them. "Yeah, um… Ty put him on the phone. The funeral is this Saturday. Any chance you can drive with me to go pay my respects to Judge Addison?"

Brian returned to undressing. "No, I'm sorry. This weekend is tight. At the practice on Saturday morning, then there's the Health & Wellness Fair planning meeting at Rise."

She took a deep breath, then blew it out. "I was hoping you would make it with me. But since you can't, I'll reserve a train ticket for Friday."

"Tracey," Brian stood up, unbuttoning his shirt. "I just can't travel this weekend, so you're not going. It's out of the question."

She placed her hands on her knees, looking up at him. "Brian—"

He swapped his button-down for a gray workout t-shirt. "Let's not make this a big thing. If I could make it, that would be fine, but I can't."

"Let me get this straight." She raised her voice. "I need your permission to travel somewhere on my own?"

"No, not in most cases. For this though, we established a guideline. You are not ever going to the Addison home by yourself."

She sighed. "I won't go by myself. I'll take Brianna with me."

He pulled on his workout shorts, then walked back over and stood by the bench. "No, I forbid it."

Tracey's skin prickled. "You forbid it? Newsflash, this is not the 1800s and I'm perfectly capable of traveling to a different state, going to a funeral, and coming back without the bad guys getting me. You're making me laugh."

"This is funny to you?"

She stood, hands planted on her hips. "Actually, it isn't, but I'm just gonna go with it, because now you sound crazy."

"I sound crazy?" He paced around, then pointed at her. "How did you suddenly forget everything we worked on in counseling?"

"None of that has anything to do with me paying my respects to a Christian man who spent his money and time making sure me and my son weren't homeless years ago."

"Like I've told you before, I have much respect for Judge Addison. But I don't want you up there around Kyle. He may be Tyler's father, but I don't trust him, and you know why."

The words slipped from her tongue and into the air before she could catch them. "If you wanted to punch that man for trying to get close to me once, you could have done it then. But oh, I'm sorry, I guess you forgot about that while we were waiting to find out if another woman was having your baby."

Brian's face turned ten hues of brown and purple. "I'm going to ignore that comment because you're not fighting fair now, and you know it. I need to get out of here and have my workout before I say something I can't take back."

Tracey said, "I'm an adult. You don't need to stop me from traveling. You can trust me."

"Trust the woman hiding texts on her phone?"

Now who wasn't fighting fair? This was a hard place to be. But at least she didn't sling any glasses at him this time.

"I wasn't hiding anything," she said between clenched teeth. "Did you ever think the only reason those texts were still on there was because there wasn't anything to hide?"

Brian moved in so close she could smell Mentos on his breath. His voice, loud and clear.

"No, because my wife had no business texting her ex-man about anything!"

The rumble in his tone brought tears to her eyes. She placed a hand on her rounded belly. Through blurred vision, she watched as he stared at her for a moment before he turned and left the room. Heavy footsteps as he stalked through the hallway and down the staircase.

Tracey eased back down on the bench.

Brianna appeared in the doorway. "Mom?"

"Yes, Brianna."

"Why did Daddy run out of here? I don't like it when he yells." Worry lines appeared on her forehead, her skin reddened. "Are you fighting?"

Tracey waved her daughter over to sit next to her. "We had to talk about something hard."

"Is he mad because Tyler doesn't live here anymore or visit?"

"No, that's not it," she sniffed. "We love Tyler and we cared for him for a long time. But he's older now and he made a choice to live with his father's family, and we support his decision."

"Oh."

"I need you to pray for your brother. His grandfather passed away early this morning. He died."

Brianna looked down at her feet. "Can I draw him a card?"

"That's a good idea." Tracey hugged her daughter around the shoulders. "As a matter of fact, you can go in your room and do that now. When you're done, pull out some comfy clothes you might want to wear after school on Friday. And put a Sunday dress and some shoes with it. We're going to visit your brother and his family."

Brianna leaned over and kissed Tracey's cheek before sprinting out of the room.

Tracey crossed her arms. Forbid her to go to a funeral? Brian must have lost his mind. So Brianna could absolutely go put her clothes together, because there was no way Tracey would leave her behind this time.

She pushed herself up from the bench, walked out of the master bedroom and over to Tyler's old room. Inside the empty space, she studied the walls. This room had never been a nursery before, and the walls boasted a strong navy-blue paint. Since she and Brian had no idea if they were having a boy or a girl, she would have to plan a neutral colored bedroom for their new little one. That meant having everything repainted, new window dressings, new carpeting, and more.

Judge Addison had passed away, and her husband was dead set against her attending the funeral. She shook her head as she ran a hand over the windowsill. Insane. Just plain nuts.

She should be choosing new baby furniture and calling painters.

Not making plans to rebel against Brian.

DO *you want your marriage to get better or worse?*

It always came back to that. No matter what type of disagreement passed between Tracey and her husband, she still returned to Pastor Downes' words from years ago.

Always with the same answer.

A resounding *better*.

But if she took Brianna and attended Judge Addison's funeral against Brian's wishes, that action alone could drive a wedge called *worse* right through the middle of their relationship. A relationship they had worked long and hard to restore.

Tracey wiped a bead of sweat from her brow as she reached down and picked up Brianna's discarded shoes and uniform from her school day. On her way to the hamper, she glanced down at Brianna's table and spied the handwritten greeting card she had created for Tyler. The scene featured a grassy green knoll and a sky full of clouds, with one ray of yellow sunshine peeking through. Inside, she'd written *I love you. God is still shining on you through the cloudy day.*

"Like my card?" Brianna strolled into the room. Her lavender robe was wrapped tightly around her, and when she stood next to her mother, Tracey got a whiff of strawberry-scented body wash.

"I love your card." Tracey hugged her. "Tyler will too."

She pointed to her chair. "Did I pull out the right clothes?"

Tracey glanced at the pile of clothing. She'd done a great job with her choices. Too bad she wouldn't need them.

"I'm sorry, but I changed my mind. We aren't traveling to New York this weekend after all."

Brianna poked out her lip. "But you said we needed to see Tyler?"

Tracey sighed. Anything she would attempt to explain to her daughter, no way would she understand it. "We do. But for now, we'll have to use FaceTime," she said, keeping the truth as simple as possible.

"Can we mail the card tomorrow?"

"Absolutely, and if you could draw one for Mrs. Addison as well, that would be super. We'll drop them in the mailbox on the way to school." Tracey turned toward the bed. "Ready for bed now?"

Brianna nodded as she took off her robe and slid beneath the covers. "I'm tired. Is Dad going to be here to say goodnight to me?"

"I don't know. But if he comes back in the next thirty minutes, I'll send him in here. Deal?"

"Deal."

She kissed Brianna goodnight, flicked on the nightlight, and shut the door behind her as she left.

If Brian wasn't back, Tracey would sit downstairs and wait for him. No fussing or fighting. She only wanted to talk this time.

When she reached the bottom of the stairs, she spied him stretched out on the couch in the living room, his hands spread over his eyes. When had he come in? She and Brianna had eaten dinner alone, and by the time Brianna took her evening bath, he still hadn't arrived. He must have slipped into the house as Tracey tucked Brianna in and kissed her goodnight.

Tracey padded in slow, not wanting to disrupt the quiet. She sat down in the leather chair closest to the fireplace.

"Brian."

He removed his hands from his face. "Yeah."

"Thaddeus and Celeste Addison supported me when I didn't have a place to live, or a decent way to support myself and my son. They kept a roof over my head when I applied for some assistance. They helped with money for groceries and supplies until the assistance came through and kept helping even after I enrolled Ty in daycare and finished my degree."

"I know all that." He said, weariness in his voice.

"Good. But what you might not realize is they never once asked me to pay them back. Not once in almost twenty years. Lots of Christians talk a good game about helping others. Judge and Mrs. Addison? They walked it."

Tracey stood up then to move closer to the couch where her husband lay.

"I said a bunch of stuff to you earlier, and some of it was unfair on purpose. I shouldn't have done that. Our past issues are dead and buried and they need to stay that way." She sighed. "So, tomorrow morning, I'll go online to send sympathy flowers over to the Addison's on our behalf. I'll call Tyler and tell him I won't make it."

She turned to leave, then glanced back. "Brianna wants you to kiss her goodnight. This is her favorite part of the day, so please take a moment to love on her."

Brian remained silent.

Tracey left the room and climbed the stairs to the second floor. Before she reached the landing, baby Jones shifted in her mid-section, sending tiny flutters across her abdomen.

She bent her head and whispered. "You hold on, little baby. I promise you, everything's going to be all right. It might not be okay, but it's going to be all right."

❧

"There's no way you can make it?" Tyler asked.

Tracey sat in front of her laptop that morning, scanning the FTD website for sympathy flowers. She kept her phone on speaker as she spoke with her son.

"No, and I'm sorry about that." She bit her lip, reading descriptions, trying to select the best bouquet. "Timing, and I'm pregnant and sometimes I don't feel well. I'm here for you in spirit and any time you need me, I'm only a call away."

"Yeah, all right." He said, his tone sharp.

"Hey!" She stopped looking at the site. "I'm picking up on something from you…"

"Brian had something to do with this?"

"I never said that."

"You didn't have to," Tyler answered with disgust in his voice. "I can read between the lines. Let me guess, he can't make it because he's busy, so you can't be here?"

Tracey sighed as she rested her back on the office chair. Why lie? What was the point? "No, he can't escort me. I'm sorry."

Tyler mumbled. "Yeah, me too. Sorry he keeps taking people away from me."

"Excuse me?"

"I gotta get this off my chest. Since I was seven years old, from you it's been Brian this and Brian that. Brian pays our bills, and Brian bought us a house, and I should be thankful to Brian because he's a good man who prays for me and supports me."

Where was all this coming from? "Ty, watch your mouth! Right now."

"No, maybe you need to listen to me this time!"

Tracey took her phone off speaker mode and moved it to her ear.

"Mom, I can still remember when it was just you and me. Yeah, I was only a little guy, but we were doing all right. I know Dad used to come visit us in our apartment. He would come see my football games and take us to dinner and for ice cream. I loved those weekends when he would play with me and put me to bed at night. Then it all stopped because you met Brian at church, and he was a doctor, and he wanted you, so you sent Dad away."

"That's how you remember it? I sent your father away?"

"That's what he said."

Kyle! Uh-uh. No. She needed to clear this up, pronto. "Okay, that's a lie, or else he remembers things differently. You're right, he used to come visit, but that was years after we broke up, when we were trying to co-parent. And I did not send him away. We had a connection, but not a commitment."

"Mom, you had me."

Tracey rubbed her forehead. For the love of God, why must he bring this up now?

"All right, Tyler, look, for your sake, neither I, nor your dad would want to rehash everything that went down between us. I'll care about him until the day I die, but when I met Brian, I knew he was my husband. Not a boyfriend. Not a baby daddy. A real life partner. If you can't see that, then you need to look a little closer."

"Okay. I'll look closer after I bury my grandpop and my mom's nowhere around for me to hug, because she's too concerned about her husband."

Tracey needed to stop the conversation. Right now. "Tyler. I'll talk to you later."

"Talk to you."

She ended the call and sat still for the next few minutes. Her son? Completely disrespectful but yelling at him wouldn't help. He was disappointed and grieving, and probably lashing out at everyone.

Kyle! Why did he pump his son's head full of fantasies? Like he and Tracey could have *actually* had a family. Maybe they could have, if she had been willing to accept a non-Christian, part-time husband with a collection of females on the side. But that wouldn't have happened either, because even though he had a son, Kyle wasn't the marrying kind. He preferred his women three ways: beautiful, accommodating, and temporary.

Tracey took a deep breath and held it for seven counts. She blew it out slow for another seven counts. Something needed to settle between the three men, but it couldn't as long as Tyler believed every single story Kyle told him. Lord, please give Tyler, Kyle, and Brian some peace and understanding for one another.

Facing her laptop, she scrolled through the FTD site once more. The Spirited Grace Lily bouquet was breathtaking. She chose that one, entering the funeral home information and credit card number. The flowers would arrive right on time for the service on Saturday.

The Lord understood Tracey wanted to be there. But He also knew she made a commitment to honor her husband. Sometimes obedience meant casualties.

This was one of them.

Brian's car in the driveway? On a Friday morning?

Tracey unlocked the back door, stepped into the kitchen, and saw Brian sitting at the kitchen island. She'd just dropped Brianna off at school. Something must have gone wrong at practice for him to be in the house at this time.

"What's going on?" She put her purse down on a stool. "Something wrong at work?"

"No, everything's fine," he waved her over. "Come on, come sit next to me."

She slid onto the seat closest to him.

He reached out and took her hand. "Judge Addison was there for you when you needed him. I stood in front of God and your family and I made vows to stand by your side no matter what, and I failed this week. I prayed about that. This is a time of grief for my family, and I need to stand up for you all. So, I made arrangements."

"For?"

"You, me, and Brianna, we have reservations at The Garden City Hotel for the weekend. We can pick her up early and go."

"But your appointments? The health fair?"

Brian shrugged. "Dan and Ruthie, they've got me covered. Dr. Blackshear can put me on speakerphone during the meeting at Rise, so I can hear the details. My family comes first. You…Tyler…Brianna. You are my family."

"I don't know what to say." She put a hand on his knee. "I wanted to be there, but I really didn't want to go anywhere without you."

"Well, you don't have to. I'm here today and I'm by your side through the weekend. Anywhere you need to go, I'll take you. You should give Tyler a call and let him know we'll be at the funeral."

Tracey stood and put her arms around his shoulders. "I appreciate this more than you can ever know."

"Now you can pull out those clothes Brianna had put away and put them back in her travel bag."

"How'd you know about that?"

He rubbed Tracey's arms. "You know that girl lives to chatter. She mentioned it yesterday when I gave her breakfast. I don't want to fight about it, though. It's all right."

And it was.

A FEELING of déjà vu washed over Tracey that Friday afternoon as she stepped from Brian's car over to the sidewalk outside of the Addison home. Wide green manicured lawn. Blooming flower beds in vivid, living color. A beautiful house. Although Tracey couldn't see it from where she stood on the walkway, she envisioned Ms. Celeste's overflowing herb garden in the back. Tracey still remembered the touch of the moist, dark earth beneath her fingertips.

Brian took her hand. "How are you doing after the ride?" He shut the car door. "You had your eyes closed for the last half hour."

"It's hot for September. Feels more like August." Tracey fanned herself as a wave of nausea passed. "I'll be okay, I guess. Just need to get to a bathroom."

"Let's get you inside then."

Brianna came up to her then, taking her hand. "Tyler's in there?"

"He should be."

"He's rich now?"

Tracey chuckled. "Not quite, he's still a college student. But he does live here."

At the front door, Brianna rang the doorbell as Tracey and Brian stood back waiting. When Tyler opened it, Tracey watched as a smile spread across his face.

"You made it! Hey, hey Paris!" He turned to call behind him. "My family's here!"

Tyler's cutie-pie girlfriend strolled over as he stood back and let them in.

Tracey opened her arms for a hug. "Good to finally meet you in person, Paris."

"Same here. He talks about you all the time."

Tracey pointed to her husband. "This is Tyler's stepfather, Dr. Brian Jones. Brian, this is Paris Mears."

"Nice to meet you, Paris." Brian said, stepping forward and shaking her hand.

"Likewise."

Tyler reached down and hoisted Brianna up into his arms. "And this is my bighead sister, Brianna. What's up, bighead!"

Brianna wrapped her skinny arms around his shoulders. "Eww, your hair too bushy. You need a haircut!"

"Yeah, all right. And you need to get taller, shrimpie." Tyler ran a hand over her head as he set her back down on the floor.

Tracey peeked down the hallway. "Where's your grandmother?"

Tyler pointed around the corner. "She's in the main living room with my aunts and uncles. Come on, I'll walk you over."

Holding Brian's hand as Tyler led them through the house, Tracey couldn't help marveling how things had changed so fast. Only a few years ago, her son was thinner and clean shaven, and with smaller shoulders. Now, he walked ahead of her in confidence, with stronger, wide shoulders and a deeper voice. He lived on Long Island and managed his own work and school details. He even had a dedicated girlfriend. From boy to man. Just like that.

When they reached the formal living room, Tracey spied Ms. Celeste, sitting in an antique chair in the corner. Her relatives surrounded her, sitting on chairs and sofas throughout the room. With her hands on her lap, and a kind look on her face, she appeared at peace, despite her circumstances. She looked up and Tracey caught her eye.

"Well, hello," she said, waving a hand. "Please come in, come in. I'm so glad you made it."

Tracey pushed past her family and made a beeline directly to Ms. Celeste. She leaned down, giving the woman a warm hug.

"I'm so sorry," Tracey said as she straightened up. "I love you, and I'm praying for all of you."

Ms. Celeste patted her hand. "Thank you and I love you too, but you listen, there's no need to be sorry about an incredible man who went to meet his Lord after a long life. I don't want any tears, and no dark colors tomorrow, okay?"

Tracey nodded. "Okay."

"Everyone, this is my grandson's family. They just arrived here from Philadelphia." Ms. Celeste announced before introducing all the people in the room. Quite an impressive group.

There was Judge Addison's older brother, Samuel F. Addison, a retired U.S. Air Force Chaplain, his wife, Victoria, and their son and daughter.

Seated closest to Celeste was Dorothy Addison-Mowry, Judge Addison's younger sister, who maintained a partnership in her law firm in Connecticut.

Across the room, on the loveseat, was Judge Addison's youngest brother, James Andrew Addison, a retired business executive, and his wife, Barbara, who was a scientist. They'd recently arrived from North Carolina.

After Tracey exchanged greetings with everyone, Tyler arrived at her elbow, whispering in her ear. "Dad won't leave his room."

"What?" She turned and whispered back.

"He won't leave his room." Tyler mouthed.

Tracey looked up. Brian was engaged in a conversation with Samuel Addison. Brianna was nowhere to be found. She probably walked off with Paris.

"Come on." Tracey stepped with Tyler over to the kitchen, out of earshot from the formal living room. She put a hand on his shoulder. "Now what are you telling me?"

"My dad won't leave his room. He hasn't moved all day long."

"Did you try to talk with him?"

"For a little while, then our people and food and flowers started coming. Me and Paris have been managing traffic for Grandmom."

Tracey nodded. "You're good for doing that."

"Can you go see about him?"

She took a step backwards. "Uh-uh. Absolutely not! That is *not* my job."

"Well, someone needs to do something. I can't even get him to say anything."

"Tyler," she rubbed her hands together. "This is your father. He needs you to encourage him."

"What do I say?"

Tracey thought for a second. "You open his door, walk in there, and tell him what a wonderful father he had. That his father loved him with all his heart. Then tell him that even though he's grieving, he needs to get up, stand up, and know that whether he recognizes it or not, God is with Him."

"What else?"

"Give him a hug and tell him how much you love him. Pray with him. Support him. Then stay by his side until he's ready to move."

Tyler cracked his knuckles, nodding as she spoke. When she finished, he turned toward the hallway.

Tracey watched him as he walked away. She'd raised a man. Part of being a man meant handling his pain as well as he managed his achievements and trusting God with everything else.

Tyler needed to be the one who held up Kyle.

❦

The next day, instead of the black blouse and skirt she'd planned to put on, Tracey wore a gauzy pink floral maternity dress to Judge Addison's funeral. No dark colors at the homegoing. Ms. Celeste's rule.

Brianna sat down in a pew toward the middle of the beautiful church. Tracey kissed her daughter, then Brian took Tracey's hand and helped her to the choir loft. Kyle and his mother had wanted her to sing, and Tracey obliged. She nodded her hellos to the choir and shook hands with the choir director before taking her seat at the end of the row.

Love you, she mouthed to Brian when he settled in the pew next to Brianna.

He nodded and winked, then mouthed a *love you too* right back.

Brianna rolled her eyes, then hid her face behind a church fan.

For the next twenty minutes, the church filled with friends, family, church members, neighbors, and community leaders. By the time Tracey spied the funeral processional vehicles parking outside the window, the old-fashioned building had people seated and standing from wall to wall. Everyone there to pay their respects to a man who had lived his life well.

The organist began to play *Great Is Thy Faithfulness*, and Tracey looked up to see the Addison family proceed to the front pew. Ms. Celeste looked positively regal, wearing a pink suit, stunning hat, and pink lace heels. She held her head high as she walked to the front. Kyle walked behind her, sunglasses still shielding his eyes. Tyler, in a dark grey suit, kept his hand on his father's shoulder. The extended members of their family followed behind them, filling in the remaining space at the front of the church.

Tracey clutched a handkerchief during the entire worship service. She held on to it tight, even while she sang *It Is Well with My Soul* along with the choir. It came in handy. She had to wipe tears from her eyes as she watched her son say goodbye to his beloved grandfather. And again after Ms. Celeste placed a rose in her husband's hands, then stood back when the funeral attendants closed the casket. Thankfully, the pastor's sermon was buoyant and hopeful, leading the audience more toward laughter instead of tears.

But when the Reflections portion of the ceremony arrived, Tracey twisted the handkerchief in her hands, wishing it were two. She cried at the childhood memories, professional stories, and neighborhood tales provided by Judge Addison's family and friends. Then it was

Tracey's turn. She took a deep breath and gave a nod to Brian and Tyler, both of whom left their pews and traveled to the choir loft to help her to the podium. Each one took a hand as she walked down the small set of stairs.

She cleared her throat before speaking. "My name is Tracey Jones. But when I met Judge Thaddeus Addison, I was a young college girl dating his charming son, and my name was Tracey Watson. I came to visit the Addison's for Thanksgiving one year and Kyle and his whole family welcomed me warmly. By Christmas, I was pregnant for some reason."

The crowd laughed. Tracey peeked over at Tyler, and he had a hand over his face. Kyle had removed his sunglasses, and for the first time, his face showed a smile.

"It's a very long story, but things grew tough for me right after that. It was a dark time, but I met the Lord during that time and when Tyler was born, I prayed for help for us. I didn't know how I was going to manage being a young mother, and my relationship was over, and life seemed impossible." Tracey abandoned her handkerchief and let the tears roll down her cheeks. "The day after Tyler was born, Judge Addison walked into my hospital room, and he picked up Tyler, and he kissed him. He prayed with me and told me everything was going to be all right. Even told me stop worrying about his stupid son."

More laughter filled the room.

Tracey kept going. "The Lord's promise is to provide, and one of the ways He provides is through people. For me, Judge Thaddeus Addison will always be my example of how God works through the hearts and hands of people who love him. He and his wife, Celeste, always loved me and Tyler, from the very beginning. They funded me when I needed an apartment and they helped me get back on my feet. I managed to finish my degree. But more than that, I learned about hope in all circumstances. There's hope in new friendships, new family, great memories, and in the Lord's work even through suffering." She shifted her weight as she leaned on the podium. "I'll miss Judge Addison, and I'll remember his kindness and generosity for the rest of my life."

She turned away from the podium as people clapped, looking over to see Brian waiting at the stairs, his hands outstretched.

When she reached him, he embraced her.

"That was beautiful," he said. "Beautiful and perfect."

Tracey wiped her eyes. "The Lord provides. He always provides, and that's the most beautiful thing in the world."

CHAPTER
Twelve

TRACEY DIDN'T NEED to return to the Addison home after the repast. Judge Addison had been laid to rest at the local cemetery. The crowd from the church had paid their condolences and, in small groups, drifted away, returning to their busy lives. With Brian and Brianna by her side, Tracey could give Ms. Celeste, Tyler, and Kyle one last hug and they could drive home.

Still, something tugged at her heart. She needed to take action on it.

In the car, outside of the church, Tracey tapped Brian's hand. "Can we follow the Addison family back to their house?"

He turned the key in the ignition. "Forget something?"

"No, but I'd like to talk to Ms. Celeste before we head home."

"Okay."

"And, I'll probably need to use the bathroom again."

He laughed. "I figured that."

At the Addison home, after Tracey used the bathroom, she walked around until she located Ms. Celeste in the main kitchen, sitting at the breakfast bar. Her sister-in-law, Dorothy, served her a steaming mug of tea.

"Hey Ms. Celeste," Tracey crept around, placing her arm around the woman's shoulders.

"Tracey! Thank you for your words today. So many people needed to hear them," Ms. Celeste said, turning to her with a smile.

"It was the truth. And if I never told you directly, bless you from the bottom of my heart for all you've done for me and for Tyler."

"Bless you right on back, sugar." She pointed at Tracey's midsection. "Now don't you need to get off your feet for a while. Carrying a heavy load there."

"Yeah, this one's growing bigger every day."

"Boy or girl?"

"We didn't want to find out. We want it to be a surprise."

"You call me as soon as you give birth, okay. I want to know you are both doing fine."

"That I'll do. Take care, Ms. Celeste."

"Love you, Tracey. Take care."

Tracey headed back toward the front of the house. When she passed the patio doors, she spied Brianna on the back lawn by the pool, shoeless, kicking a soccer ball back and forth with Tyler and a few of his cousins. It looked like she was having the time of her life.

Addison family members were spread throughout the house. Main living room. Dining room. In Kyle and Tyler's living area. Tracey gave hugs and nods to a few, but she still didn't see the one person she needed to find before leaving. She traveled down further, toward the end of Kyle's wing, and there he was, outside on the side patio.

Kyle sat alone in a white Adirondack chair, his face to the concrete. Tears streamed down his face, soaking his shirt so much the fabric had turned translucent. It looked as though grief weighed his shoulders down, and pain made them shake.

Wordlessly, Tracey slipped off her heels and carried them in her hands as she retreated back into the hallway, then over to the glass doors leading out to the back of the house. She stepped onto the deck.

"Ty," she called out. "Ty!"

Tyler looked up from the soccer game. He stopped and jogged over to his mother's side.

"What's up?"

"Can you take a break and get something cold for your dad to drink? Like a ginger ale or something?"

"Where is he?"

"On the side porch. I'm going to go talk to him for a minute, so give me a few moments with him, but then bring him that drink, okay."

"All right."

Barefoot, she padded back through the house and over to the side porch again. She tapped once on the doorframe, then pushed the door open and kept going until she stood beside Kyle, still seated in the Adirondack chair.

He brought his head up and wiped at his eyes. "You…uh…you tell my mom and Tyler goodbye?"

"Yeah, I gave your mom a hug." Tracey pulled Kleenex from her purse, passing the tissues to Kyle. "Can I join you here for a minute?"

"Uh…yeah."

"I'll have to lean on this porch railing. Those chairs are nice, but they're too low for me to sit in right now."

He wiped wetness from his face. "I guess. I…I've never seen you like this."

"Like what?"

"This pregnant."

"I know, right." She sighed, peering down at her belly. "Well, I can tell you I looked this large with Tyler, but much less confident. And my maternity clothes did not come from Pea in the Pod. I had so little money then, I was lucky Goodwill sold maternity gear."

"How can you joke about that?"

"What? Me when I had Ty?"

"Yeah." Kyle balled up tissue in his hands. "Aren't you bitter? Even a little?"

Tracey shrugged. "I used to be, but it's been nearly twenty years since all that happened. I forgave you a long time ago."

"How? Why?"

"When I gave my heart to the Lord, he led me to a place of forgiveness. And your parents helped me when I needed it. Like I said today at that podium, the Lord provided."

He directed his eyes past her, to the green lawn beyond the porch. "Years ago…I know…I should have apologized for leaving you that way. Just pissed off and angry because I didn't want to be a father yet and I couldn't control what was happening. I was stupid. You needed me."

"I did. But I see it differently now. If you'd been there for me, I wouldn't have been lonely and depressed and staying with my relatives. I wouldn't have gone to that evening church service with Aunt Zee, and I wouldn't have given my life to the Lord."

Kyle stayed silent, staring at his feet. Tracey straightened up as the side door swung open and Tyler stepped onto the side porch, holding an icy glass of ginger ale. Brian followed right behind him.

With all three men in front of her, this she might as well keep talking. She might never have this opportunity again.

"Kyle, what I know is that God guides non-obviously. Do you know what I prayed for after I gave birth to Ty?"

"What?"

"I asked him to give our son a loving father."

He looked up at her. "And God gave you Brian?"

"No, God worked on your heart and you came through for your own son. You are Ty's loving father. Now Brian?" She gestured to Brian. "He's the husband I prayed for. He is Tyler's father too, but in a different way."

Fading sunlight filtered through the area, bathing the porch with a yellow orange glow. Tracey's eyes shifted from Kyle, to Tyler, to Brian, and back again.

Right now. I need to address them all.

As if she needed a reminder, right at that moment, baby Jones gave her a sharp kick in the side. She shifted her body to a different position, where she could see all three of their faces clearly. "Ty, thanks for getting the drink for your dad."

Tyler shuffled over and handed the glass to Kyle. "Yeah…uh…no problem, Mom."

"Now stay here for a minute, because I have something to say to all of you."

The men stared at her, their faces blank.

"Life is too short for misunderstandings and resentment. Either talk through everything or give it the Lord and let it go." She took a deep breath, blew it out and continued. "Tyler Addison, you've been raised well by three very loving, intelligent, strong men. Your father is a successful entrepreneur. Your stepfather is a family physician. Your grandfather was a well-respected county judge. No one took anything away from you. If anything, you received multiple blessings."

Tyler gave a slight nod. Tracey could tell he was uncomfortable, but so be it. He needed to hear this.

Next, Tracey directed her gaze to Kyle. "Kyle Addison, you gave me Tyler. Thank you, from the bottom of my heart. Because I adore this young man."

Kyle put his drink down, stood up and stepped over to embrace his son, he then let go. He remained silent but kept his arm about Tyler's shoulders.

Finally, she shifted her gaze to Brian. "Brian Jones, you are my love and my daily blessing. I'm so thankful for that, I don't have enough words to articulate it."

Like Tyler, Brian also gave a short, wordless nod. But peace filtered through his eyes. He seemed grateful she'd spoken those words in front of all of them.

Then she addressed them all again. "Judge Addison lived his life in gratitude, even after his Parkinsons diagnosis. The three of you, if you take away nothing else from this conversation, I want you to remember that."

When baby Jones kicked her in the side, shifted, then kicked her again, she smoothed her hands over her protruding middle. "I'm done talking and making you all uncomfortable, so Tyler, please go peel your sister off the back lawn. We need to go."

"Mom, can I say something, please?"

"Sure."

Tyler turned to his father, then his stepfather. "I appreciate both of you. And…I need to thank you both for raising me," he said.

Tracey beamed, looking at her grown young man.

Lesson learned. Class dismissed.

CHAPTER
Thirteen

"I need a cigarette." Tracey's mother, Alice, yawned as she spoke. "You better tell me this is the last time you doing this. You ain't no spring chicken."

"Ma, you were almost the same age when you gave birth to Jamal."

"Right. I wasn't a spring chicken, either."

"You're getting a new grand baby." Tracey moved her arm around so she wouldn't pinch her IV line. "Aren't you excited?"

Alice strolled over and peeked through the window blinds. "Eh, a little. I have more fun with my grand babies after I don't have to change their diapers. And I have the best time with them at Tyler's age." She turned back to Tracey. "I think I see a smoker's bench down there. Looks like you'll be here for a minute. Let me get a cigarette and I'll be right back."

"Fine, fine." Tracey shook her head. No point in saying anything to Alice about quitting smoking. Nicotine was her way of enjoying life.

Tracey lay in her hospital bed, trying to relax. The journey to baby Jones number two? Yet another adventure. Back when she'd given birth to Tyler, her contractions arrived fast, Aunt Zee drove her to the hospital, and Tracey pushed him out in less than an hour.

Brianna's birth was even faster. Tracey's water broke in the middle of the night and, again, the contractions seemed to jump from ten minutes to one minute in an instant. By the time Tracey and Brian arrived at the hospital, she was fully dilated, and Brianna was on her way out.

But this third baby was taking its time.

Not only was Tracey two days past her due date, but her cervix wasn't budging. Dr. McCallum recommended she be induced. If the baby wasn't on its way soon, the medical team planned to give her a C-section.

Brian returned to the hospital room, a plastic pitcher of ice water in his hands. He looked around. "Where's Ma?"

Tracey sighed. "Smoke break."

"How are you feeling?"

"I've never had to stay in bed like this before. How long will this take to work?"

"Depends. It could be a few more hours or longer."

"Great."

"Stay positive, honey." Brian placed the water on the side table, then stood by her bedside and took her hand. "Your vitals are good. The baby's vitals are good."

"C-section?"

"That's not happening unless baby Jones doesn't respond."

"And what would that mean?"

"Tracey, honey, stop, please. Just because you're having a different experience this time doesn't mean it's a bad thing. Turn it around, maybe Tyler and Brianna were way too impatient and they both tried to run out. Now this baby? It's having a nice leisurely time in there. Just chilling."

She laughed. "Just kicking back, huh?"

"Yeah. Think of it like that."

"Nah-uh, maybe your baby's just lazy. You need to tell it to come on out right now!" Charla's voice echoed off the walls.

Tracey looked up to see Charla and Ricky walking in, with little Ricky trailing along holding a trio of three small *Congratulations* balloons.

"Those are for me?" Tracey reached a hand out as little Ricky toddled over and pushed them toward her. "Thank you!"

Charla prompted him. "Now what do we say?"

"Welcome!" Little Ricky's big eyes displayed his joy.

Ricky Jones, a slightly thicker, bald version of Brian, picked up his son and held him. "This is different. You're actually in a hospital bed. When Brianna arrived, you guys were home so fast we had to visit you at the house."

"I know, right." Tracey shook her head. "Everything's different this time."

Brian walked over to his brother's side. "So, man, I heard you've been copying me again. You've been doing this since we were kids. When are you going to stop?"

Ricky shrugged and laughed. "I am not copying. It's just the way things turned out."

"What things?" Tracey furrowed her brow. "The way what turned out."

Charla opened her plaid poncho, exposing her baby bump. "The way this turned out!"

Everyone clapped, even little Ricky, who grew so excited he bounced up and down in his father's arms.

Tracey grinned. "Congratulations, both of you! What a surprise! We'll have two Jones babies back to back. Did you show the grandparents?"

"Not yet," Charla said. "We ran into them downstairs on their way to the cafeteria, but we wanted to show you both first. Brianna almost spoiled it though. She ran up to me to give me a hug, but I kept my arms out so they wouldn't see my middle."

Richard, Sr. and Marilyn Jones had arrived at the hospital less than an hour after Brian called and told them Tracey would be induced. Tracey didn't know how they managed that, coming all the way from their home in Trenton. Her in-laws must have sped all the way over. Now they were on unofficial Brianna duty until the new baby arrived.

"Hey, hey, all you people need to back away. I'm trying to get to my mom!"

Tyler? Tracey sat up and leaned over to see better. Sure enough, she spied her son walking toward the hospital bed, holding his girlfriend's hand.

"Ty!" She could hardly contain her excitement as he leaned over to hug her. "I'm speechless! How are you here?"

He squeezed her hand. "Hey, it's Sunday, and my man right here," he pointed to Brian. "He calls me and says you're being induced. I told Paris, jump in the car cause my Mom's 'bout to have the new baby."

Paris giggled, pushing her dark hair over her shoulder. "I don't even think he hung the phone up before he started the engine."

Tyler let go of Tracey's hand and walked over to Brian, giving him a strong handshake and hug. "Congratulations, man. For real, congrats and I am going to love having a new brother."

Tracey held up a hand, wincing as contraction pain hit her. "Please stop saying brother. We don't know…"

"What it is yet," Tyler finished. "I know. I'm just saying. I have a sister. It would be nice to have a brother."

"I'll take whatever God gives me." She shifted her arm once again to keep her IV line free. "He's in charge and he knows what he's doing."

❧

Five hours later, only Brian, Tracey, Dr. McCallum, and two nurses remained in Tracey's room.

Brian held both of Tracey's hands as Dr. McCallum addressed them.

"We don't want to hold off any longer. The baby's heart rate is dropping, and Mrs. Jones, your blood pressure is rising. We are prepping the operating room for a C-section. Dr. Jones?"

"Get a gown and scrub in?" Brian said.

Dr. McCallum nodded. "Yes, please. Mrs. Jones, this is your first C-section, but its routine for us. We're going to take excellent care of you and your baby, and your husband will be with you the whole time."

Tracey nodded, even as anxiety made her skin feel like static electricity pulsed through her veins instead of blood. Everything in the room seemed brighter for some reason, and her thoughts raced as the nursing team moved about her in a flurried pace, getting her ready to deliver. Brian? Yes, he was on his way to prepare for the operating room. Brianna? Her in-laws took her home to wait.

The baby? The baby would be okay, right? She'd accepted the child, and all the tests had come out fine. The heart rate dropped? Did that mean it was dying? Not now. They'd come so far. Everyone in their family, even Tyler, filled with so much joy. Everybody ready for little baby Jones to arrive in the world.

On her back, Tracey gazed at the white ceiling tiles as she rolled from her hospital room to the operating room. If the baby was moving at all, she couldn't feel it. *Baby Jones, please hold on.* The operating room felt cold, and it smelled of disinfectant. When Brian took her hand, she stared in his face. No smiles. Nothing but concern. Tracey closed her eyes.

Lord, please…just…please!

CHAPTER

Fourteen

VALENTINE'S DAY

"Please don't burn down my kitchen." Tracey said, walking through the room with her infant swaddled in her arms. "I know those kits are supposed to be foolproof, but I'll be over here in case you need me to come in and save you."

The temperature was nearly ten below zero that Valentine's Day. It had been a very cold January, so when February rolled around, Brian planned to cook a romantic holiday meal for them from Blue Apron. With Brianna staying over with a school friend that evening, it gave Tracey and Brian the perfect chance to stay inside and bond with their new little one.

Brian shook his head. He sat at the kitchen island, pulling out instructions and packaged food items from the Blue Apron box. "Woman, I got this."

"Yeah, okay."

"Lemon-dijon chicken with roasted carrots. Mm-hm. This is going to be so good you will want to spend the rest of the evening thanking me for the best Valentine's Day dinner ever."

"Oh, I would do that anyway." She kissed him on the cheek. "I'm gonna go feed this greedy one right here." She gazed down. The baby squirmed in her arms, his tiny head moving about. "Seems like all he wants to do is eat."

Brian smiled, reaching over to stroke his son's cheek. "Strong appetite. This is my boy right here."

She elbowed him. "Hey…"

"Yes, my second boy, I know. I'm a blessed man."

"Yes, you are."

"It's Valentine's Day. So…uh…I'm getting a different blessing later, right?"

"Of course." She winked at him. "I'm all yours. Now and forever."

He winked back at her. "Hot mama."

She smiled as she strolled into the family room. Sitting in the recliner, she grabbed a burp cloth from the diaper bag on the floor, then pulled a white cotton baby blanket around her shoulder. Lifting her baby and turning him, she settled him down at her breast. She helped him latch on, then relaxed with the blanket around them as he nursed. He was a chubby fellow with curly black hair and wide brown eyes.

And ever since Reginald James Thaddeus Jones entered the world, he had not once stopped warming Tracey's heart.

Leave a Review

Dear Reader,

I hope you enjoyed this story. Reviews are a wonderful way for readers to connect with authors, and they also play a crucial role in helping us spread the word about our stories.

Whether you loved the story or liked it a little, a quick review on the platform where you purchased it would be incredibly helpful. Even if you received a complimentary copy, your honest feedback is valuable.

Of course, I'd also love to hear your thoughts directly. Feel free to reach out at kl@klgilchrist.com!

Warmly,
K.L. Gilchrist

Subscribe To My Newsletter

How will you find out about my latest releases, read reviews for recommended books by other Christian fiction authors, and more? By becoming an author newsletter subscriber. You can sign up on my website at klgilchrist.com. As a gift, all newsletter subscribers receive the free short story collection *Five For The Journey: Stories*

This free eBook is only available to subscribers. So sign up today!

About the Author

K.L. Gilchrist crafts true-to-life contemporary stories for women of faith. The author of *Engaged* and other novels enjoys bringing order to chaos and dancing whenever and wherever she can. She and her family call the suburbs of Philadelphia, PA home. Visit her online at klgilchrist.com.

www.ingramcontent.com/pod-product-compliance
Lightning Source LLC
Chambersburg PA
CBHW061223210726
48294CB00006B/1954